SWORD OF FORGETTEN DREAMS

CALLIE VIERA

CONTENTS

CHAPTER I

SLUMBER'S SHADOW

"Mother! I saw something yesterday," young Ernest said to his mom as she made dinner, but she wasn't paying much attention to him. She was lost in her thoughts, remembering what had happened in the marketplace earlier in the day. Regardless, he didn't stop. He went on to tell her what he had seen.

"There was a horse, and I was walking in a beautiful place. Everything was bright and pretty like the flowers at the palace gates. Mom, are you listening?" He tugged on her dress and finally got her attention.

"Oh, son. Yes, I am listening. What were you saying again?" she asked, this time, paying more attention to him.

Smiling, Ernest continued with his story. "Then I saw a bright light from the middle of the woods. It looked like it was the source of the other light."

Ylva, Ernest's mom, was confused. Where had he seen what he was talking about? It wasn't as though they had gone anywhere the day before. However, she kept listening. Perhaps it was something from his imagination. Kids could be so silly at times.

"Okay. So, what happened to the light?" Ylva asked, smiling at him. "Did you see the source?"

"No. It wasn't a light. It was a big knife… like what the guards carry around." Ernest was trying to remember what it was called, and he tilted his head to the side. "Don't say it, Mom. I will remember the name," he assured her.

Ylva smiled. Ernest was her bundle of joy, and she couldn't imagine life without him. He was the best gift life had given her.

"Yes! It is a sword. I remember it!" he exclaimed happily, jumping around. "I remember it, Mom." And with that, he jumped into her embrace.

Ylva hugged him back. He was smart for his age, and it brought joy to her as his mother. However, she soon went still. Ylva had been happy about Ernest's progress with his studies, and she didn't think of what he was saying. A sword with a shining light? She hoped it wasn't what she was thinking…

"Where did you say you saw this?" Ylva asked, dreading his answer, and then he dropped the bomb.

"I saw it on the bed when I was sleeping yesterday, and then you came to wake me up, so I don't know what happened next." He sighed.

Ylva was terrified. A dream. Ernest's son just told her he had a dream. What other news could be as terrifying as this?

"Mom, do you know where the sword is? I want to see it. It was calling my name too. Do swords talk?" he asked, confused.

Looking around, Ylva immediately stood to close the windows of the kitchen. She also peered outside into the yard to make sure there was no one close by, and with that, she shut them all.

"Mom, what is wrong?" Ernest asked. He hadn't realized the weight of what he just told his mom.

"Can we go to see Mr. Sword?" Ernest requested eagerly. He didn't notice the look of despair on Ylva's face yet as she had her back turned to him.

"Ernest, did you tell anyone about this?" she asked, coming to crouch right in front of him and holding his hand.

The young lad was, however, confused. He couldn't understand the sudden change in the atmosphere. Why was she suddenly looking all serious?

"No, Mom. I haven't told anyone yet." Ernest couldn't wait to brag to his friends. He had visited somewhere beautiful, and a knife, which they'd always known to be inanimate, had spoken to him.

"Now, listen to me carefully," Ylva started, holding his hands. "You must not tell anyone about this or else bad things will happen. Do you want bad things to happen to me and you?"

Ernest didn't understand what was happening, but still, he shook his head. He didn't want anything to happen to them.

"Good boy. So, don't tell anyone. Is that clear?" Ylva asked again and he replied affirmatively.

Ernest never understood why his mom fretted so much that evening… at least not until the bad things really happened and he had grown and matured.

On the day he lost his mom, Ernest had another dream when he slept in the middle of the day. It was a little different from the first one, and he told his friend about it. He was too young to realize his mom had meant all dreams.

That day, just as he expected, Ernest's friends were fascinated. Their eyes wrinkled with delight and they listened with rapt attention. It didn't take long for Ernest's story to spread, and soon, they got a visit from the Dreamcatcher.

Ernest had seen them first through the window, then he excitedly went to tell his mom. The most elite workers of Dream Haven were visiting their abode.

"Mom, the Dreamcatchers are here," he told her and watched all the color drain from her face. He was surprised at how quickly her demeanor changed. She had just been laughing a few minutes ago.

Just as quickly as he told her, Ylva peeped through the window, and truly, the Dreamcatchers were around. She feared Ernest had mentioned something about his dream to an outsider.

"Ernest, did you tell anyone about what you saw when sleeping?" she asked, shaken. Ylva hadn't told him it was called a dream. After all, the word was banned among commoners in Dream Haven.

The commoners of Dream Haven were not allowed to dream or say anything about it. Dreaming was meant only for the elites, and it was sacred. Dreaming or talking about them was seen as an act of rebelling.

Since their house was located on the outskirts, there were still quite a few steps before the Dreamcatchers got to their house, so Ylva had the chance to arrange some things.

"I saw something else and I told my friends," Ernest replied meekly. He hadn't realized the gravity of what he had done, but he sure knew what the look on his mom's face was—despair.

Ylva knew she couldn't scold him at that moment, so she hugged him and opened an underground hideout. Ernest never knew it existed, and Ylva always prayed she would never need to use it.

For an underground, it was pretty bright and stylish. However, it did not end there. There were various fruits and food—enough to feed a grown adult for at least five years.

"Wow!" Ernest exclaimed. "I like this place, Mom." He smiled at her, and Ylva forced out a smile too. However, there was no more time.

"Ernest, I need to tell you something. You are a very special kid, and it has brought me more than enough joy to have you as my son. You are made for greatness, and I have always wished I would be here for you at any time, but it seems we have to part ways here."

"Mom, why are you crying?" Ernest asked, wiping the tears

that rolled down Ylva's cheeks. He couldn't understand the sudden change of mood. Everything had been fine.

"They are happy tears," Ylva lied. She didn't want Ernest's memories of what could be her last moments to haunt him for life.

"Ernest, do not tell anyone about anything you see. The world is filled with bad people and they might try to hurt you if they know you have a gift. So, do not tell anyone, okay?"

Ernest nodded carefully. At this point, he was scared. His mom was being weird and unlike her usual self. "Are the Dreamcatchers bad people?"

Ylva didn't reply to his question. Instead, she continued with what she was saying. She needed to round up as quickly as she could, otherwise, everything would be in vain.

"Mom is going to have a little talk with them, so don't come out of this place, alright? All I want you to do is read and count. If you get hungry, you can eat too. Okay?" she said.

"But, Mom, I'm scared. Why won't you stay with me?" he asked, holding on tight to her arm. It looked like he would begin to cry any second now.

"I'm not leaving you. I only have to talk to them, then I'll return. Okay? Don't cry, baby. Everything will be fine. Do not come outside or say anything, no matter what you hear, okay? Mom loves you so much."

And with that, Ylva ushered Ernest into the hideout. She prayed for his safety and went back to shelling melon seeds like nothing had happened.

About two minutes later, Ernest could hear his mom's voice, though not clearly. It seemed like the Dreamcatchers were around and she was speaking to them.

For a while, it sounded like they argued, but then everything went silent and he heard footsteps retreat. However, Ernest neither stood from where he sat nor did he leave the underground hideout.

Just as his mom had made him promise, all he did was sit without coming out for nine years. And when he did, he was 15 years old.

With fear, Ernest woke from his sleep. It was the same dream that haunted him for the past years. When he finally stepped out of the hideout, he understood all that had happened that evening, and he blamed himself. He was so stupid.

Ylva was nowhere to be found. The Dreamcatchers had most likely come for him that day, but he had hidden, so they took his mom and executed her as a traitor. If only he hadn't told anyone about his ability to dream… maybe Ylva could still be here.

Ernest stood from his bed and put on his shirt. It was almost midday, and he was just getting up. However, he wasn't bothered. He was going to keep living in hiding like he had for those nine years. And yes, he wasn't going to dream or have ambition. All he would do was idle around until death came for him too.

Without dwelling much on the dream, Ernest headed for the river. He wanted to take a bath in an open area today, then he could go on to the market square and see the state of the town. It was the best place to get information.

Just as he had planned, Ernest began his day by visiting the nearby river for a bath, then he took dried persimmon for breakfast and headed for the market.

On his way, he had to pass through the Dreamcatcher's hearth, however, he was determined to avoid them at all costs, so he instead made a detour and took a longer route. He was neither a six-year-old boy nor a 15-year-old. Ernest was 20, but he was somewhat stuck in the past.

Ylva had told him to live, but here he was only surviving. Every day felt like torture. He needed to isolate himself from others, and he couldn't trust anyone. To him, everyone who approached him had a reason, which could be good or bad. But Ernest concluded their reasons were bad, so he had no friends. He was all alone and on his own without looking or wishing to change that side of himself.

Soon, Ernest got to the market and it was scanty. It seemed as though everyone decided to ditch the market today. Ernest had no guess what he could have missed, but he soon found out.

"Excuse me, why is it so scanty here today?" he asked a young guy walking around. It was one of the few times he had spoken to anyone since he got out of the hideout. All those years, he became used to talking to a hand latch his mom had woven for him. To him, it was a piece of her, and it was his home.

With curiosity, the man turned to look at him. He was surprised there was someone around who didn't know about the schedule for the day. The news of the agenda was everywhere, and only a visitor wouldn't know. However, Ernest looked like a local.

"Have you been living under a rock?" the guy asked, and Ernest turned back. However, there was no one behind him. It was just him and the guy. He would later get to know him as Frederick.

"Excuse me, I only asked a question." Ernest couldn't understand Frederick's condescending reply. It pissed him off.

Usually, Ernest would have turned away, but he was annoyed. Frederick didn't look any older than him, and he had no idea why he was being rude.

"Well, I only asked a question too, and as usual, it is the gods doing new things and predicting life again," Frederick replied with his chest puffed. It looked like he was trying to pick a fight, which was the last thing Ernest wanted.

Shaking his head, Ernest turned away from Frederick and headed to the main town. He could hear drums like there was a celebration, and he wanted to know what the occasion was. He promised himself not to do anything even though he heard the mock in Frederick's tone.

Regretting that he had asked Frederick a question, he began his journey following the sounds.

Frederick, on the other hand, also felt a little guilty for taking out his annoyance on someone else. A stranger at that.

Frederick had some private issues he was going through, and it was affecting him. It was all in relation to the Dreamcatchers too. He hated the fact that they decided everything that went on in town without thinking of others.

Here in Dream Haven, no one was allowed to dream or hope. They all had their lives mapped out by the Dreamcatchers, and going against them would mean rebelling. Frederick had grown up following the rules just like his family and others, but it didn't take long for him to get fed up.

He couldn't go on with it any longer, so he was going to rewrite the destiny they had planned out for him. He wasn't going to just sit around anymore. Someone needed to give others hope, and he would gladly do that, even if no one supported his point of view.

On his way, Ernest thought about Frederick. He sounded pissed about the gods, and he wondered what he meant by that. 'Could he be referring to the Dreamcatchers?' he wondered but shook his head.

No one in their sane mind would say something like that about the Dreamcatchers. It would be considered blasphemous, and it incurred a death sentence. Execution before everyone, and the head would be hung for everyone to see. It would serve as a warning.

Soon, Ernest got to the venue and made his way through the crowd and to the front of the stage. It was the Dreamcatchers like he guessed, and he shook his head at Frederick's recklessness. He must either be ready to die, not scared of dying, or out of his mind. Ernest decided it must be the last option.

The Dreamcatchers were dressed in their ceremonial wears, and the security around was tight. Ernest knew he was being reckless. Since everything that happened 14 years ago, he had never come this close to a Dreamcatcher, let alone a group of them. However, he wanted to see what was happening.

The chief sorcerer sat on a carpet with four other junior ones standing behind him and holding incense pots. Right before the sorcerer was a bigger pot, and he was burning some powder and twigs. Ernest wondered what they were, but he didn't have to do that for long.

There was a lady behind him, and noticing the questioning look on his face, she gave him an answer.

"It's the yearly sacrifice and Thanksgiving for the God of Dreams. They are going to thank Morpheus for looking over us all."

Ernest didn't realize that he scoffed. Thanksgiving indeed. However, he didn't say anything. Instead, he just watched the priest do his things. However, the lady didn't stop there, she had more information to give.

"Also, they will be introducing new dreamers today, and… ah! There will be prophecies too."

Ernest then turned to look at the lady. She was young and pretty. However, she didn't sound or look excited about the whole thing. It seemed like she had another reason for being there.

"Prophecies?" Ernest asked. It was the first word he had said since he joined the crowd.

"Yes. I'm Pearlie." She smiled at him, stretching out her hand for a shake.

Ernest couldn't understand why she was being so welcoming, but he shook her hand skeptically.

"Ernest."

"Nice to meet you, Ernest." Now, her smile was wider, and Ernest felt his body shudder. She was being weird and he didn't reply. He didn't know anything about her and felt it would be creepy to say the same to her.

"So, why are you here? Are you happy to be on the stage?" Pearlie asked like it was the most normal thing in the world.

'Is she crazy?' Ernest thought. Didn't she see he was nothing but a commoner?

"I do not understand your questions. Aren't commoners supposed to be here?" he asked, raising his brows.

"Oh, yeah. That's true. You just look like someone with a gift," Pearlie whispered for only his ears, and Ernest immediately glanced around. He hoped no one heard what she just said. With him being surrounded by Dreamcatchers, the last thing he wanted was to draw attention to himself.

Pretending not to have heard what she said, Ernest immediately left the crowd and headed for home. He was glad Pearlie wasn't following him.

Upon getting home, Ernest took off his shirt and sprawled on the bed. He couldn't remember the last time he had spent so much time around that many people. He reminisced on the two weirdos he had encountered earlier in the day, and with that, he thought about what Pearlie had said.

In some ways, her last question had him wondering... 'Why wasn't he on the stage too? And why weren't they allowed to dream? Why did it have to be a form of rebelling to dream?' He had a lot of questions, but there were no answers.

Ernest knew he was gifted, and his mom, heavens bless, confirmed it. However, he lived in constant fear and was unable to act for himself. He always had to hide, and it was because of those who had destroyed his family. The Dreamcatchers. All the painful memories came back, and he drifted to sleep with a heavy heart.

In his sleep, Ernest dreamed. It had been a long time since he had this particular dream, but still, it was familiar.

CHAPTER 2

PEARLIE'S PROPOSITION

Ernest couldn't remember the details from the first time he had the dream, however, he knew everything was more defined and clearer.

In the dream, just like the first time, Ernest was walking in an open space filled with beautiful flowers. However, unlike the first time, the flowers looked wild as if they hadn't been tended to for a while. Nonetheless, he didn't stop. Instead, he kept walking, occasionally reaching out to touch the beautiful flowers.

Soon, Ernest came to a woman. He was surprised to meet a being, but she didn't talk. All she did was point to a far distance, and he began walking in that direction. Just like she didn't say anything, he didn't ask either.

After walking for a while, Ernest came to a stream. The water was unbelievably clear, and he squealed with delight. He had never seen anything so beautiful in all his years of existence. However, as he bent to scoop some of the water, the stream disappeared, and he was standing on something that looked like a mall, and all his surroundings changed.

A confused Ernest stood, observing his environment. What

just happened? And how did he get teleported? It felt very real and unlike a dream.

However, he soon found the area familiar. He had been here once before… in the first dream he had when he was six. The dream where he had seen the dazzling sword that spoke.

Since he knew the direction, Ernest began walking just like he had 14 years ago. However, unlike before, there was no dazzling light. The forest was dim and all he could hear were eerie sounds.

Still, Ernest didn't stop. He kept on moving, and soon, he found the sword. Immediately, he got closer to it, and it began to glow again. However, Ernest wasn't blinded. He could see everything clearly.

"I've been waiting for your revival."

Ernest turned around. It was the sword speaking, and he wanted to laugh. It seemed like he was going crazy.

After Ernest had his first dream, his mom, Ylva, tried to convince him that it was all in his imagination and there was no inanimate object that could speak. Back then, he believed her as she easily talked him out of it, and as he grew, he agreed with her even more. There was no way a weird person would talk. They weren't in a fairy tale.

Little did Ernest know though… he was living a fairy tale as the main character. The hero. And on his shoulders rested the fate of a kingdom and its people's freedom.

Shaking his head, Ernest wanted to believe that he was hearing impossible things, but the sword spoke again.

"Do not try to convince yourself otherwise. I'm the one speaking, and I brought you here."

"Show yourself!" Ernest demanded, swinging his arm in the air. "I want to see who you are."

"I am the one. The Sword of Forgotten Dreams."

Ernest froze. He had heard of that before. It was from the folklore his mom told him. However, as he grew, he had always thought of it as a myth. If it really existed, why was there so much suffering in the land?

"I do not believe you. The people have been suffering for years, and nothing has changed, but you expect me to believe the Sword of Forgotten Dreams is real? You're saying it is not a legend?" Ernest asked, frustrated.

"It is all real, and you are the reason everything is like this."

The sword's voice was unbelievably calm, and it felt like he was taking his time to talk. Ernest wished he could have him still everything at once.

"It was all you. You were supposed to protect everyone and make sure the power of dreams was not misused, but instead, you disappeared. You left everyone to suffer under the unjust Dreamcatchers, but now, you blame me for your shortcomings."

Now, Ernest was panting and annoyed. Wasn't the Sword of Forgotten Dreams supposed to be mythical? If it was true, why wasn't it living up to its name?

"You forgot, Ernest. I am nothing but a tool, and if my bearer doesn't come for me, I would be of no use."

Ernest thought about it. The Sword of Forgotten Dreams was right. But where was its bearer? Did something happen to him?

"How about your bearer? Where is he? How has he been able to turn a blind eye all this time?"

"He lost hope and the will to live. So, he hasn't come for me, and I can barely reach him. Ernest, will you continue to live in the dark?"

It was now that Ernest realized he was the bearer. Truly, he had lost hope and the desire to dream. What everyone was going through was all his fault.

All his life, after what happened with his mom, he lost the will to do anything and only stayed alive because his mom had sacrificed herself. He had been so weak, and this also affected the Sword of Forgotten Dreams, causing its light to dim.

"So, what would you have me do?" Ernest asked, disappointed in himself.

"Be a hero, our hero, and dream again. Renew your dreams as they are valid and for us all. Only then can you bring us all out of this misfortune."

And with that, Ernest woke up. His body was covered with perspiration even though it was winter.

For some time, Ernest lay there, allowing his dream to sink in. All this time, he had remained silent and did nothing. However, he didn't know his life wasn't for him alone. Because of his silence, many had died and suffered all through the years, and he wasn't just going to sit around anymore. He had to start from somewhere.

For the first time in years, Ernest didn't just eat scraps. Instead, he made a sumptuous meal for himself and had a feast. His mom had sacrificed herself, so the least he could do was make everything worth it.

Seeing how it was dark in the world of the Sword of Forgotten Dreams, Ernest deduced the sword could most likely disappear or become a myth if he didn't revive himself for everyone.

Ernest had chicken as a part of his breakfast. It was one of his favorites before the death of his mom, and after everything, he stopped eating things he loved as a way of punishing himself.

However, after what he had seen at the Dreamcatcher's Thanksgiving yesterday, and in his dream today, he didn't want to be a bystander any longer. He was going to do all he could.

With this in mind, his mind drifted on to Pearlie. With the way she had looked at him and commented, he guessed she knew something. However, he couldn't just draw conclusions. He had to find her first and maybe then he could get some information.

Ernest had no plans for the day, so he decided to start something immediately. He put on his shirt and headed for the market. If he wanted to find anyone or anything, the market was his best bet.

Ernest stepped out of the house, and unlike other days, he actually wanted to be outside. He noticed everything on the streets, and somehow, he was at peace with himself in a way he couldn't explain.

Soon, Ernest got to the market, and as usual, it was bustling. There were various products and marketers with pretty and eye-catching products. However, Ernest wasn't there for any of those. All he wanted was to find someone.

"Looking for something?" Ernest heard a female voice just beside him, and he almost jumped out of his skin. Who was it that couldn't maintain a healthy distance?

"You scared me!" Ernest exclaimed, seeing who it was—Pearlie. She showed up at the right time.

"Sorry about that," she apologized, but it didn't look like she meant it. "We meet again." With that, she flashed him a cheeky smile.

Ernest cleared his throat. Seeing her now, he wasn't sure what to say. "Yeah, we do."

"Well then, do you want to check out my goods?" Pearlie asked. However, she didn't wait for him to reply as she immediately dragged him to her stall.

"I never knew you were a merchant," he said, and Pearlie shrugged.

"Of course, there are many things you do not know about me and... well, everything."

On getting to her stall, Ernest noticed there were no customers, and he wasn't really surprised. She didn't sit with her goods, and they didn't look all that enticing either.

"What are you thinking of?" Pearlie asked Ernest, but he didn't reply. Instead, he asked another question.

"Who are you?"

Pearlie laughed. Ernest's question intrigued her. "I'm a merchant, of course."

But Ernest shook his head. He was sure there was something more, so he probed further. "What do you sell?"

"Now, dear, that's the right question. I am a dream merchant, and I help people find their way."

Immediately after she said this, Ernest glanced around and checked that no one had heard them. Why was she being so reckless?

"Are you crazy?" he seethed. "Do you want to get us killed?"

However, Pearlie only smiled. Now, Ernest was beginning to believe something was truly wrong with her.

"Don't worry. Those words are for your ears alone." And with that, she told him more about herself.

"I am a dream merchant, and I have the responsibility of helping the bearer of the Sword of Forgotten Dreams get back on his feet. I am to help him in fulfilling the prophecy.

Ernest could feel the rate of his heart quicken. She knew about him and his dreams. It was the reason why she had approached him and spoken about him climbing onto the stage yesterday.

Ernest tried to hide his surprise, but it was obvious on his face, and Pearlie shot him a knowing look. He wasn't imagining anything. There was someone who knew of his existence in Dream Haven.

"How do you know me?" Ernest finally asked. He couldn't keep his questions to himself any longer. He needed to speak to someone. Only then would he get more information, and at the moment, Pearlie was looking like the perfect person.

"The prophecy, dear. You are the hero spoken of in the prophecy, and I was right to wait. I knew you would surely come."

Ernest found it awkward that she was talking to him so informally, however, he said nothing. The last person who did that was his mom.

"When was the last time you had a dream?" Pearlie probed, staring straight into his eyes.

"Last night." Ernest's reply was solemn, but he was excited. He never imagined he would be able to talk to anyone about his dream.

But here he was telling it to a stranger. Well, she didn't feel like a stranger anymore. Pearlie nodded, and he took that as his cue to continue. Perhaps she would be able to explain the dream to him.

"In my dream, I was walking through a forest and came across a dazzling stream, and afterward, I found a map. It was all confusing because I soon found myself before the Sword of Forgotten Dreams. Everything happened very fast, and honestly, I do not understand or know where to start."

Ernest sighed and looked at Pearlie with hopeful eyes. He hoped she could offer him some help and, at the same time, important information.

Throughout his explanation, Pearlie didn't say anything, and when he finally paused, she nodded. Afterward, she drew the cloth, covering some of her goods, and took out a small chest.

"Open it."

And that was exactly what Ernest did. Inside the chest was a scroll, and it contained the drawing of a map. For a few seconds, he went through and studied it, and upon realization, his eyes widened.

"Is it what I think it is? he asked, unsure, and Pearlie nodded.

"Yes, it is the map you saw in your dreams, and it is going to lead you to the Sword of Forgotten Dreams. Ernest, you are truly the bearer of the sword, and only you can free the people of all their sufferings and tribulations. It has to be done by no one but you."

"But why me?" Ernest was unsure. He didn't think he could do it. Ever since the death of his mom, he had always blamed himself for everything and wallowed in self-pity. To Ernest, it didn't make sense that someone like him would have to do such an important thing.

"Because it has to be you. The sword has chosen you and appeared in your dream. Not only that, but you are also the hero spoken of in the prophecy, and the map agreed. If it's not you, the chest wouldn't have opened, and you wouldn't be able to retrieve its content."

"But…"

"There are no *buts,* Ernest. It is high time you stopped wallowing in self-pity and lived up to your destiny. Only you can do this. Of course, you will find helpers and a team, but you need to lead them."

Ernest passed for a while and thought of all that Pearlie had said. Could everything be up to him? He wasn't sure he could do it. He had given up on dreaming a long time ago, and it was surely going to be hard to start again.

"Where do I start?" Ernest asked Pearlie and she let out a laugh. However, he didn't understand why. He was asking an important question, and all she did was laugh. It confused him.

"You have to find the answer yourself, young warlord. Everything is within you—only you can find the answers."

Even though Ernest stood and watched her with pleading eyes, Pearlie didn't say anything more. She had carried out her part in his destiny. At least, for now.

Before Ernest got the chance to ask another question, Pearlie began to pack up her things. She had done her part, and there were no more reasons to stay.

"Where are you going?" Ernest asked, horrified. Didn't she say she would help him in his quest? Surely, that couldn't be all the help she was going to offer him. He hoped it wasn't because there was surely no way he would be able to get started all by himself. He needed extra hands to make this work.

"Returning home, dear. Other things await me."

"Wait… I thought you said you were to help me in my quest?" Frustration was etched on his face.

"Yes, and I have done that. At least, for now, I have done my part. The rest of this lies in your hands. You need to find the answers. They are within you."

All Ernest wanted to do was scream. He couldn't understand why she kept hammering on the fact that he had the answers within him when he couldn't think of anything.

"You have to be focused and reflect, then the answers will come to you. But I have a gift for you. I will help you meet one of your team members, and both of you will join together to do great things together."

Hearing the last part, Ernest heaved a grateful sigh. At least she wasn't leaving him all alone. She had some conscience left within her.

"Thank you." And with that, Ernest helped her with the goods. He didn't need to ask her why she was leaving the market so early. She had perhaps been waiting for him, and being a merchant was all a facade.

"So, how did you know I was going to come looking for you?" Ernest asked. He remembered she mentioned it earlier, but he wasn't paying attention.

"My instinct does not lie, and when you reach a stage in life, there are some things you get to know."

Listening to her answer caused Ernest to laugh. Why was she speaking like an old folk who had seen it all?

"Why do you like to speak like an old folk? You don't look any older than me."

With this, Pearlie cackled. "There is more to what the eye sees, young warlord."

The look on Pearlie's face told Ernest she wasn't joking. Was she perhaps a witch? He remembered she had mentioned him being a prophet countless times. Yesterday, she also tried explaining what the sorcerer was doing.

"Are you a witch or perhaps a sorcerer?" Ernest's question was straightforward. He wanted to know what and who she was without mincing words.

"You can address me in any way you feel sounds right." The

conversation ended there, but still, Ernest followed her. After all, she had promised to lead him to one of his team members.

As they walked, Ernest thought about everything that had happened over the last 24 hours. He would never have guessed his life would take such a turn after meeting a person and having a dream.

"But why do you think the forest where the Sword of Forgotten Dreams lies is dim? The first time I visited—sorry, I mean had a dream—it was incredibly bright there, and the flowers were in their bloom."

Pearlie heaved a sigh. "The forest is a reflection of yourself. It mirrors how you're feeling and your attitude to life. When was the first time you had the dream?"

"About 14 years ago if I'm not mistaken."

Nodding, Pearlie began explaining to him, "You see, back then, your attitude to life must have been different. Perhaps you had hopes for the future and you weren't afraid to imagine the future to be better. But now, I do not think that is the case. You seem to have a lot of doubts about yourself, and you shut yourself away from the world. You became a hermit who viewed life as grim and gray."

Ernest understood what she meant. Everything she had said so far was true. Ever since the Dreamcatchers visited him and his mom that day 14 years ago, something changed in him.

At first, Ernest didn't understand why such a thing had to happen to him. However, as he grew, he understood better, and he blamed himself. Everything had happened because of him. If only he hadn't told his dream to his friends… the Dreamcatchers would not have visited them, and he would still be with his mom today.

Since then, he had thought of himself as bad luck. He hadn't even met his father. He thought, perhaps if he stayed away from everyone, his terrible luck wouldn't rub off on them.

Worse still, there was no one he could speak to, and it seemed everyone had forgotten about him and his mom when he got out of the underground hideout years later. He blamed the world for everything, but he had no idea he was the key, and he was broken. He needed to gain closure and heal.

"Do you think I can do this?" Ernest asked Pearlie for the umpteenth time.

"The answer lies within you, young warlord."

Ernest sighed. He should have guessed that would be her answer. However, Pearlie wasn't done. She soon added, "But, I believe you can. The prophecy has never been wrong, and it has always chosen the right man for the job. So, I do not think you are making the wrong choice. You shall find your way and make things right."

CHAPTER 3

THE RELUCTANT ALLIANCE

Pearlie's words seemed to have reassured Ernest, and he calmed down a bit. Perhaps, embarking on the journey to find the Sword of Forgotten Dreams and liberating the people wasn't such a bad idea.

All he had to do was trust in his abilities and make things work. After all, he was the chosen one—the one singled out in the prophecy.

Ernest promised himself not to dwell much on the future anymore. He would now take things as they came and be steady on his mission. Nothing would go wrong that way. He would not sit idly and watch as a bystander doing nothing anymore.

They had been walking for a while now, and Pearlie did not look like she was prepared to stop. Instead, her pace only became faster.

"Aren't we there yet?" Ernest asked as he tried to match her pace—she was incredibly fast. He was still curious to learn more about her, but it seemed as though Pearlie would not reveal anything.

"Not yet, young warlord. Keep your balls calm," she said with a chuckle.

For the rest of their journey, they walked in silence. Ernest thought about the turn of things, and Pearlie thought about the past, wondering what the future had in store.

"Ernest?" someone called and he turned back to look. It caught him by surprise. Over the years, Ernest had never shared his name with anyone. Who was this person? It definitely had to be someone from his past.

"Ernest? Is that really you?" the person asked again, and he tried to remember where he had seen the person, but his brain did not recognize them.

"I am sorry, but who are you?" Ernest asked, and the person immediately ran to him and enveloped him in a hug.

It was a young man around his age, and Ernest feared it was one of his mates from when he was younger. He did not think anyone would recognize him. However, if there was any, his mates from back then were his best bet.

"It's Finn," the guy finally said and Ernest froze.

He glanced at Pearlie, who had a questioning look on her face. She was interested to know who the stranger was.

"Who is he?" she mouthed, and Ernest whispered to her. He wasn't sure how he should react to the reunion.

"I missed you. Where have you been all this time?" Finn asked with curiosity, and Ernest felt a bit reluctant to give an answer.

Back then, Ernest was not really close with Finn, so he wasn't expecting this much excitement from him. Also, they had grown up and everything had changed. He knew Finn would have realized what it was that happened back then, and he was sure that was a good thing.

Someone knew about his existence and his gift. Worse still, they reunited when things were about to take a new turn... when he wanted to become intentional with fulfilling his destiny.

Regarding Finn's comment about missing him, Ernest said nothing. He wasn't sure how to reply. Plus, one of his mates was the one that had ratted him out, and he couldn't say he trusted anyone. He wasn't a naive child anymore.

"I have just been here and there." Ernest smiled politely. He wasn't sure how to react with the way Finn was clinging to him.

At first, he wanted to pretend Finn had the wrong person, but he'd answered to the name, and the locket he had since childhood was still around his neck. Even if he denied it, he was sure Finn would still press on. So, he decided to tell the truth. Moreover, he would be setting out on the mission to find the Sword of Forgotten Dreams soon.

Pearlie did not like Finn either. She could feel like he was being fake, and he wasn't being true to his words. However, she did not make any comments. She only hoped Ernest would be smart enough to discard him. They needed to keep moving.

"Are you going somewhere?" Finn asked, staring at the stuff in Ernest's arms. He wanted to see what was in them and did not acknowledge Pearlie's presence.

'So rude,' Pearlie thought with a slight scowl appearing on her face.

"Yeah. I can't see anyone downtown," Ernest lied. He wasn't sure where he was going as Pearlie hadn't told him, and even if he was, he did not think he wanted to share his location with Finn. They were meeting for the first time in years, so he wasn't sure what sort of person he was.

Knowing Finn would most likely ask for his location or address, Ernest decided to beat him to it. The last thing he wanted was for his location to be leaked.

"Where do you stay? You know, we could meet up sometime, and when I am returning from downtown, I could come to yours so we can catch up."

Finn's face lit up and he nodded.

Ernest's suggestion was smooth, and Finn readily accepted. He did not ask for Ernest's address and apologized for delaying his journey.

"So, he is a friend?" Pearlie asked. She wanted to know what Ernest thought of Finn.

"Umm… kind of. We used to be friends before everything, you know. I never would have guessed anyone would recognize me."

Pearlie nodded. "He must be very good with faces to have recognized you after all this time."

"Yeah. I guess. Where are we going?" he asked Pearlie and she smiled.

"Downtown, of course. She wasn't joking when she told him the answers were within him and all he had to do was find them. However, Pearlie did not realize his powers were as strong as they were. It seemed as though he could predict the future in some ways, and she couldn't wait for him to reach his maximum potential.

"Here we are," Pearlie announced as soon as they reached a clearing. There was only one house around, and in some ways, it reminded him of his own house.

Ernest hadn't seen the person, but he felt they could work together. After all, it was said that your house or where you live reveals what kind of person you are. However, Ernest wasn't prepared for who he saw next.

"Hello, Frederick," Pearlie called out for the young lad, wanting to know if he was inside.

Almost immediately, a reply came. It was Frederick, and with that, Pearlie went inside.

Frederick was the first on the list of team members, and so far, he was the only one Pearlie knew. Ernest would have to find the others and win them over himself. Perhaps, with the help of Frederick too.

"Wait here, I will be back in a bit," Pearlie said, and with that, she went indoors. She wanted to give Frederick a brief on the situation. Ernest only nodded.

It took a few minutes before Pearlie and Frederick emerged from the house. Ernest could hear them laugh and he nodded. It seemed as though everything had gone well, and he hoped he would not have a problem with Frederick.

Because he was bored, Ernest had walked closer to the fishpond in the yard and watched the fish swim, so he had his back to Frederick and Pearlie. However, he was surprised to see Frederick upon turning back.

"You?" they both said simultaneously. While Ernest stood with his hands on his waist, Frederick ran his right hand through his hair.

"I see you guys have crossed paths before." Pearlie smiled. However, the lads did not look like they wanted to breathe in the same environment for another minute.

"Is he the lad from the prophecy you talked about?" Frederick asked Pearlie.

He hoped she would say no, but of course, he knew better. Just before they came out, she had told him she came with the young warlord, and of course, Frederick knew she would not bring just anyone over to his place. But still, he said silent prayers in his heart and prayed.

Pearlie nodded with a smile. Judging from their countenances, she knew they weren't pleased to see each other, but she acted like it was the most iconic meeting she'd ever witnessed.

"No, I do not think I will be able to work with him. He can't be my teammate. I want someone else." Ernest agreed. Seeing how Frederick had lashed out at him on their first meeting, he did not think he could work with someone so violent. He didn't want someone who couldn't keep his emotions in check.

Frederick, on the other hand, thought of Ernest as completely unserious and not up to the task. Where had he been all this time while everything was crumbling? He had done nothing but watch everyone suffer, and now, he suddenly wanted to play hero?

He remembered the first time they met. However, he didn't think Ernest did. That day, Ernest had left the comfort of his home as usual and wanted to check for any news in town.

However, he came across an injustice but didn't say anything or try to stop it. Instead, he just passed like nothing concerned him.

Frederick was very disappointed in his behavior. Although Frederic didn't dwell on it, he had gotten pissed off when Ernest asked him questions in the market that day. He felt annoyed that someone with a lack of sense for justice would deem him fit as the right person to ask a question. It annoyed him to no end.

However, just like Fredric thought, Ernest did not remember this. To him, their first time meeting was on Thanksgiving and Sacrifice Day. He didn't recognize Frederick from any other experience.

"Well, I am glad to see you are on the same page. I think you guys will get along quite well."

The duo turned to face Pearlie in shock. How could she say that after seeing the looks on their faces?

However, she didn't spare any of them a glance.

"The land is in turmoil, and every day, the suffering of the people intensifies. However, the two people who can bring us out of this aren't doing a thing. Instead, they are at loggerheads with each other, claiming not to be interested in working together."

Ernest and Frederick looked like they wanted to argue more, but instead, they swallowed their distaste. After all, the least they could do was grant each other the benefit of the doubt and lead the land and its people to salvation.

"Let us just get along with each other." And with that, they shook hands, making Pearlie smile. Her eyes twinkling with mischief and satisfaction. The first phase was done.

"So, I will leave you guys to get acquainted." Pearlie handed the chest containing the scroll back to Ernest.

"This will lead you to the Sword of Forgotten Dreams, and I hope you can get this done without hitches. I wish you all the luck the world has to offer."

Hesitantly, Ernest took the chest from her. Somehow, he felt like Pearlie was mistaken. How could he do something so great? He shook his head.

"I do not think I can do this," Ernest protested, and Frederick shook his head. It seemed as though the lad wasn't ready for this. Why was he the chosen one of all people?

"I cannot read and understand the map. How am I supposed to know where to find the sword?" He was frustrated, and somehow, Frederick sympathized with him. Why was he so unsure of himself?

Frederick was very young when he knew what he wanted, and his role in the prophecy. He was born prepared, and his family made sure he studied right from birth. Was it all because of this? At first, he did not understand why he was brought up that way, but these days, it was becoming clearer.

"I can help with that. I am good with the map."

Ernest smiled. "Thank you."

"I think my work is done here. At least for now." And with that, Pearlie turned to leave.

"Wait... why are you leaving so soon? What if I—sorry, we— need your help?" Ernest asked. He was not sure he wanted Pearlie to leave, and since Frederick had promised to help, he realized it was better he began to address them as a team.

"Well, young warlord, we have spoken about the main things, and I don't think there is anything you cannot do yourself for now. However, if you need my help, you can find me. The map will lead you to me."

Without another word, Pearlie turned and left. This time around, no one stopped her. Not even Ernest.

"So, where do we start?" Frederick asked, watching Pearlie's retreating figure. He was prepared beforehand, and only needed Ernest to say the words.

"I say we set out now. The faster we get this done, the quicker it all gets solved."

Frederick nodded. He had no issues with that. "I will just pick up a few things then."

Frederick ushered Ernest inside, and while he packed his backpack, Ernest looked around.

It appeared as if Frederick lived alone, but still, the house looked as homey as it could. At first, Ernest wanted to ask Frederick about himself, but he decided against it. He wasn't sure what sort of stories he had, and Ernest wouldn't want to open old wounds if there were any. So, he kept his questions to himself. After all, they could always get to know each other during their mission.

"I think…" Ernest was about to make a comment, but Frederick hushed him, pointing at the door. It seemed as though they had some visitors, and they weren't wanted ones.

Frederick was a little surprised. He had chosen this spot because he wanted to stay away from people as much as he could, and he couldn't work out why someone would come here.

Glancing at Ernest, Frederick shook his head. 'Could it be that Ernest's location and abilities have been leaked?'

Tiptoeing, Frederick walked closer to the door and peeked through a hole in it. Just like he had guessed, there were Dreamcatchers outside and a commoner was with them.

"Did you tell anyone you were coming here?" Frederick mouthed.

Ernest began to shake his head, but then he remembered Finn. Just like Frederick, he tiptoed and stared out through the tiny hole. There, he saw Finn.

"That little…" Ernest swore under his breath, and Frederick realized it meant he recognized someone from the group.

Looking around, he noticed that there were just three. Perfect, he could easily take them on or they would leave if he told them Ernest wasn't around.

*Go out through the backdoor, I will meet you in a bit." And with that, Ernest's fear came back.

He remembered what happened 14 years ago. It was the same way his mom had told him to stay in hiding and she would come to get him, but she never did. He had to live in the hideout for years, and he came out to discover she wasn't alive anymore. She had been killed.

No, he wasn't going to allow something like that to happen again. Not under his watch. If anything happened to Frederick on his account, Ernest wasn't sure how he was going to live. It would be tough.

"What are you waiting for?" Frederick seethed.

"No, I am not leaving without you," Ernest declared.

Frederick couldn't help but facepalm himself. 'Why is he being difficult?'

"I said I will meet you in a few minutes. What part of that do you not understand?"

All these words were spoken under hushed tones. They were being careful enough not to be heard by the Dreamcatchers, but they soon broke down the door.

"Gracious heavens!" Frederick swore. How were they supposed to get out of this now? "Can you use a sword?"

But Ernest's reply was negative. He couldn't use a sword. Frederick wanted to hit him, but he fought the urge. Instead, he decided it was better to face the Dreamcatchers.

Just like when he had checked through the hole, there were only three, and given Frederick's skills and strength, it didn't take him more than a few minutes to get them down. However, he didn't knock Finn out. He only tied him to a chair and left Ernest to do his thing.

"Let me go, you bastard!" Finn swore, but Frederick paid him no attention and only went on to continue packing his bag.

"Finn, I thought you claimed to have missed me and were excited to see me. Why have you called the Dreamcatchers on me?"

Ernest's voice was icily cold as he stared at Finn.

Finn laughed. "You are still as foolish as you were back then. You tell everyone your shit and assume everyone likes you and wants the best for you, but life is not lived that way. At least not here in Dream Haven."

Ernest felt his legs wobble, but he did his best to keep standing.

"In case you haven't figured it out, I was the one who called the Dreamcatchers on you 14 years ago. Why do you have to be the one with a gift?" he asked rhetorically.

"You told the Dreamcatchers about the dream I had?" Ernest asked and Finn let out another burst of wicked laughter.

"Yes, I did." He sounded like he was daring Ernest to do something to him.

Immediately, Ernest slapped him across the face. Finn was the idiot who contributed to the death of his mom. All this time, Frederick didn't say anything. He was done with packing up and only watched the duo.

Finn had an inferior complex, and immediately when he got home that day, he had cried asking his parents why he didn't have such a gift. Unlike Ernest back then, he knew about dreams and how important they were.

Also, he had the mentality of destroying things he couldn't have while growing up. His parents had imbibed that in him, and they went on to report Ernest to the authorities. They knew hearing Ernest wasn't around anymore would please their child greatly, so they took him out.

CHAPTER 4

THIEF IN THE NIGHT

Frederick watched as Ernest's face contorted in anger, his breathing labored, and his fists clenched by his side. Clearly, the slap was too little to show the full magnitude of his emotions.

Finn looked up to meet Ernest's gaze. His cheek, bearing the handprint of his slap, throbbed pink. He smiled at Ernest, "Do you feel better now?" he said with spite, knowing that more Dreamcatchers would be there any minute now. Ernest took a step forward, ready to engage in an all-out brawl against his childhood friend.

A heavy hand on his shoulder restrained him, and as expected, it was Frederick's.

"We don't have time for this. I'm sure the reinforcements are on their way here."

Ernest's steps didn't falter as he kept walking towards Finn. He wanted to kill him. The pain of the betrayal was fresh in his mind as he remembered the day his mother died. If he could turn back time, he would have never told Finn of his dreams. Heck, he wouldn't have told anyone.

He grabbed Finn by the scruff of his neck, screaming and

punching him until his knuckles bled. "What did I do to you? Why did you hate me so much? My mom was nothing but kind to you."

Back in the day, whenever Ylva came to pick Ernest up from school, she would come bearing gifts or snacks. She never came empty-handed, and she had particularly paid attention to Finn. After all, he sat the closest to Ernest. Sometimes, she would pack him lunch together with Ernest's.

However, everything went sour and she lost her life. Ernest still blamed himself. If only he hadn't told anyone about his dream. But then, there was no way to rewind time.

Glancing in between Ernest, Finn, and the bounded Dreamcatchers, Frederick walked across the room to stare out the window, and just like he had guessed, he could see more Dreamcatchers from afar. They would soon be here, and it would be risky if he didn't make an exit with Ernest.

Glancing swiftly around the room, Frederick's eyes searched for something to use to escape their impending plight, and his eyes soon landed on the lantern at the edge of the room.

He walked over to the lantern and picked it up. Fire—that was it. He was going to start a fire and distract the Dreamcatchers, and then they would make their exit. But he needed more oil.

Without wasting time, Frederick picked up the oil bottle and began to sprinkle it around the room. He was careful enough not to get the oil on Finn or the Dreamcatchers he had knocked out.

It didn't take long for him to do this, and he pulled Ernest off from Finn, whose face was now a bloody mess. Blood dripped from Ernest's hands and the youth panted heavily from the physical strain. Picking up his backpack with his other hand, Frederick threw the lantern to a corner of the room. It didn't take long for the blazing fire to spread.

Frederick grabbed Ernest, who was in a daze, by his arm. He was watching Finn's face dripping with blood, but they needed to leave immediately. Kicking the door open, he noticed their closest neighbors rushing over with buckets of water to douse the fire.

The bounded Dreamcatchers woke from the shouts and heat from the fire. However, just like Finn, it was hard for them to get out of the burning house. They had been tied together, and Finn could not move in his chair. So, all they did was scream, hoping someone would come to their rescue.

The reinforcements were much closer now, and they stared at the crowd emerging with buckets of water in confusion. Using the commotion as leverage, Frederick and Ernest made a getaway without drawing attention to themselves. All they did was blend into the crowd.

They went back to Pearlie. Her home offered them comfort as she tended to Ernest. However, they needed to leave as quickly as possible as they could not stay there for long. They had a quest waiting to be completed.

Ernest looked at the gentle fire giving him warmth, its flames filling the room with soft crackles as it burnt the wood, offering him a semblance of peace. The warmth reminded him of his mother's embrace.

Sobs racked his body, remembering the day he lost her. He still could not believe that it was his friend who caused the greatest loss of his life.

Pearlie walked into the room, her soft steps both silent and heavy, with a fresh bowl of water and bandages for his fists. She set them down on the nearby table as she took her seat beside him. She grabbed his hand tenderly, wiping the blood away with warm water and a cloth.

"Frederick told me what happened, and I'm sorry to hear that. It must have been quite a shock for you. I hope you find comfort in the path that lay before you. Many find different things. I hope you find what you need." Pearlie patted Ernest on the back and tears rolled down his cheeks.

They fell into a comfortable silence. His mind going back to the gentle cackling of the fire. His eyes followed it this time, watching the embers rise and then disappear a few feet above the flames.

He missed his mom so much. He would never forgive Finn or his family. They had ruined his life, and it was with this in mind that he fell asleep.

Ernest woke up to being shaken by Frederick. The sun was just rising, casting an ethereal light into the room. The flames had long since burnt up the wooden fuel as it was just ash that remained. Ernest packed his bags and pulled on his tunic, careful not to disturb his bound knuckles. He met Frederick standing in the doorway.

The young men exchanged pleasantries and made their way to Pearlie. They bid her goodbye and were soon on their way. They had to set out early, and she gave them a few things to aid their journey.

At some point, there was a crowd gathered around what appeared to be a fight. However, Ernest was familiar with this situation. It was all planned out and orchestrated by thieves who wished to steal from the unsuspecting spectators.

As the crowd howled and cheered for either party, thieves would go around picking the pockets of innocent viewers and robbing them of their valuables.

Ernest grabbed Frederick's arm and shook his head. They had a quest, and watching meaningless fights was not a part of it. However, Frederick was less concerned with Ernest's displeasure and made his way to the cheering crowd. He wanted to see what the fight was all about.

Dismissing Ernest's warning, he pushed the crowd to get a better view. Two men clad in simple linen trousers were rolling on the ground. At one point, the one with longer hair was at the top and gained the upper hand in the fight, but soon, the other would be winning.

Frederick wasn't sure who to cheer for. In his eyes, the fight seemed pretty balanced, and the men had matching strengths.

Soon, Frederick felt a slight nudge behind him, but he didn't pay any attention. He guessed it was one of the spectators who tried to get a better view. However, he still went on to check for his pouch. Alas, he had been robbed of his belongings and his bag was torn open.

His eyes stared frantically as his posture betrayed surprise and anger. Pushing his way out of the crowd, Frederick searched for who could have pickpocketed him and soon noticed a petite figure snake around the crowd with eyes on him, the rest of the face was covered. It looked like a little boy, and immediately, they made eye contact before the boy ran off.

Ernest hurried after Frederick, who was chasing the boy. The boy weaved around the crumpled marketplace with masterful skills. Frederick, losing ground trying to avoid the crowd and many stalls, bumped into people, knocking them to the ground.

Ernest was faring better as he was used to running through the streets in avoidance of someone. He was catching up to the thief, who turned a sharp corner running up some stairs that led up to a hill. He did not know this part of town. It was riddled with thieves and scum that he wasn't familiar with.

Soon, Frederick caught up to him and passed. He didn't wait and was oblivious to the danger ahead. Cursing to himself, Ernest ran up the stairs behind him. Of course, he couldn't leave him alone.

The chase on the stairs lasted a few minutes until they caught the thief branching off into a corner. They followed the thief, running as fast as possible, and they could feel their bones get tired, however, they didn't stop. They couldn't afford to.

The thief led them to a branch of tightly woven paths, some heading up the hill, some heading back down. It was clear that the boy's intention was to cut them off his tail.

Unknown to him, Frederick was masterful at tracking. He would not lose the boy's trail.

Reba pulled off and had successfully gotten away from the two young men who chased her. They never found her in the labyrinth as that was her territory and she ruled supreme.

Chuckling to herself, she pulled out the little pouch that contained a good amount of coin. Jiggling it against her ear, she knew she had caught a good one. She walked toward home—one she had once shared with her teacher.

Smiling, she knew she could feed herself for many weeks to come with the coins and wouldn't have to go out hunting for a while. However, danger was looming, and without warning, a large arm grabbed her from behind and pushed her against the wall.

Frederick looked into the green eyes of the young woman. A small frame gave the appearance of a boy. He was fooled. But now that he observed her, it made more sense. She had a light touch and quick feet. Looking closely, he noticed a crossbow strapped to her thigh and throwing daggers to her waist.

"Did you really have to take us the longer route?" Ernest asked between pants. He had just caught up with Frederick.

Glancing at the face of the human Frederick grabbed, Ernest's eyes widened. He never would have guessed it was a female.

"Hand the pouch over and we will let you go," Ernest tried bargaining. But the smirk on her face confused him.

"Or what?" Her reply caught them off guard, and they shared a glance.

Looking at the larger man who pinned her to the wall, Reba smiled at him, confusing Frederick for a moment. She kicked at his knees and pulled his arm down towards her chest level, pulling the arm behind him and straddling his back. She had him in a difficult hold.

Frederick yelled out in pain, his eyes darting to Ernest and back to his assailant. He couldn't believe she had him in this position, and he blamed himself for letting down his guard. He thought of her as a harmless little lady.

"I'll tell you what... I'll keep the coin and be kind enough to let your friend go. I'm not this nice usually, but it's a bright day today and I feel good."

Ernest put his hands in front of him and walked slowly towards them, showing that he meant no harm.

"I am Ernest, and the man over there is Frederick. Nice to meet you. Can we stay with you for the night?" he asked, hoping his charm and friendly demeanor would convince the thief to help them, and Frederick was just as confused.

"Why do you think I would do that?" she asked. "For all I know, you could be from the rival gang, or hired killers."

Reba lived a dangerous life and she wasn't about to let her guard down for strangers.

"We are not killers, and I assure you we are not from any rival gangs or anything of the kind. We're trying to find something of great importance and we just need a place to stay away from the eyes of the Dreamcatchers."

Ernest knew he was taking a risk by mentioning the Dreamcatchers, but he did so anyway. His instinct told him she was to be trusted, and he didn't doubt it. After all, Pearlie had told him the answers were within him.

Reba hated the Dreamcatchers and wanted them gone. Finding a common ground, she looked at Frederick, whose face was pink from straining.

"Come with me. You see, anyone who hates the Dreamcatchers is a friend of mine. Just like the enemy of my enemy is my friend."

With that said, Reba led them to a secluded cottage that had a strange building on top of it. Seeing the design of the house, Frederick guessed she used the top building for long-range focuses as crossbow was her primary weapon. They could use someone like her on their mission. She would surely be useful.

Reba led them through the small doors, forcing them to duck as they entered. The house was clearly not created for individuals with their height, especially Frederick's in mind. The decor of the house was quite simple on the inside, and it reminded Ernest of the underground he had lived in for most of his life.

With a table, a chair, a bed in the distance, a fireplace to serve as a kitchen, windows facing outwards and stairs leading up to the roof, it served as a simple yet efficient defense. She turned the chair towards the table, pulled out a stool and yet another chair. Then she gestured to the men, asking them to sit. Reba lowered herself to the stool, pulling it towards the fireplace, and began sharpening her blades.

"So, tell me, why do you have the Dreamcatchers on your case?" she asked nonchalantly.

"Is there anyone in Dream Haven that is free from the Dreamcatchers? There's no way you can escape them."

Peeking up at him through a curtain of her hair, Reba gave Ernest a knowing smile. He was right with what he had just said. Chuckling to herself, Reba turned her attention to the burly young man named Frederick.

Frederick gazed around the small cottage, wondering to himself how anyone could live in such a small space. His long arms would not allow him to do so.

Ernest gently nudged him in their host's direction. She smiled, pointing at him with a small blade. He was a fine specimen.

The one called Frederick would fetch a much larger price than the smaller one called Ernest. She further debated who to sell them to in her mind. Surviving the winter was a harsh challenge. Her eyes sized them up again and she decided she would call Zayn.

Once the night fell, Reba decided she would make her way to Zayn's territory. She smiled at her own thoughts. Ernest noticed the look on her face and he did not like it. It was similar to the look that merchants gave when sizing up goods.

Ernest felt he had made a mistake by trusting her. Perhaps the best thing to do was retrieve the pouch and go on their way.

Reba smiled again, and Ernest felt uncomfortable. Her smiles were becoming creepy, and he lowered his head to avoid her gaze. They needed to leave this place as soon as possible.

"I will be right back. There is something I have to check on." With that, Reba stopped sharpening her knife and stepped out.

Immediately, Ernest nudged Frederick, who was still fascinated with the little cottage.

"Something isn't right, and we have to leave tonight," he whispered.

"If we ever hope to make it out of Dream Haven alive. The Dreamcatchers must have combed through half of the slums, searching for us. You know how strict they are with the dreams."

Reba stalked the door and eavesdropped on their conversation. She wouldn't like to get herself involved with the Dreamcatchers, and she had no strength to deal with them. But if perhaps she sold them to Zayn, then he would deal with her problem and she could keep the money she got from the sale to herself. However, for some reason, she kept doubting whether selling them was the right thing to do.

From what she heard them say, they had a map in their possession, and the map was to lead them to the sword of something. She didn't quite hear that last part.

Maps were very expensive when sold to the right buyer. But swords were more expensive, so she busted open through the door. She had to join them on this.

"I will come with you," she declared.

Ernest shot her a confused look. 'She must have been listening to our conversation,' he thought to himself.

"And why do you think we would trust someone who deems it right to eavesdrop on our conversation and take her on an important journey?" He almost sounded like a knight.

'He will not turn me down,' Reba thought, smiling to herself.

"I have always hoped to leave Dream Haven one day. Perhaps you guys are my ticket out of here, and besides, I fancy a quest too if it brings so much more coloring to my dull and real life." She bounced on her feet, barely containing her excitement. Frederick glanced at Ernest, seeking his approval. Ernest thought that this way, they would have an extra fighter.

He stretched out his arm, offering a shake. "We have an agreement then."

Looking at him squarely in the eye, Reba stretched out her arm and shook his hand.

"Of course we do." Reba had a sultry smile on her face. Then they planned their next movements for the day and gathered supplies that night.

Reba called a few of her underlings, ordering them to keep the peace in her absence. She told them she had no idea how long she would be gone, but that they should not allow the rivals to trespass into her territory.

She looked up at the gates of the city. She had never been this close to it. Its size dwarfed her easily. She took her first step into the strange adventure.

CHAPTER 5

DREAMSCAPE DANGERS

Reba asked herself for the thousandth time why she thought going on a quest was fun. She grimaced as she pulled her leg from the muddy terrain just a couple of leagues outside the south gate of Dream Haven. They called it The Willowing Marshlands.

"It should have been called The Sticky Mosquito if you ask me," she remarked dryly as she swatted away a swarm of mosquitoes that dared to suck her dry. It looked like the men were not having it easy either.

The knight was struggling to hold up his broad sword on his head, careful so it would not fall into the messy bog. Ernest, with only a bag, somehow managed to make it look graceful as he dragged his slim body through the mud.

"If we keep going this way, I'm sure we will make it out of here by sundown. I hear it's not just mosquitoes that feast on blood." Frederick deliberately ignored her comment, and Reba didn't say anything else as she was tired from all the hiking.

The thought of having her blood sucked out of her left her face scrunched in disgust. Frederick turned to look at her face, exploding with laughter at her expression. The group continued their muddy journey through the marshlands.

Ernest looked behind him to see Dream Haven slowly disappearing in the distance. Bidding goodbye to the home he had known all his life, he knew he would return. But for now, thinking about Dream Haven only brought him pain and anguish. He had lost a lot.

It was finally sunset when they made it to a stream that marked the end of the muddy journey. They all heaved a sigh of relief and washed their bodies clean of the mud.

The only problem was that, on the map, it said the rain and erosion had caused a stream before them to grow into a small river. Frederick stepped forward, judging the depth of the water.

"I can't say how deep it is. Can you guys swim?" he asked them. They didn't have the luxury of time, otherwise, he would have suggested building a boat.

"I can. Just a bit though." It had been a while since she last swam.

He turned to Ernest, raising his eyebrow in a questioning manner. "Just a bit too."

Frederick shook his head, alarmed at his fate. He would not let them die in a baby river.

"I will go across and then throw that branch you see over there," he said, pointing to a large fallen branch. "And then I'll pull you to me," he added. After laying down his bags and the sword, he took a tentative step into the water.

He had directed that Ernest would carry his sword while he would carry his own bags. He stepped slowly at first into the water, judging its depth to be at about his waist, which meant Reba would be nearly submerged.

The height of the water was not of concern. It was the current. He possessed the lower body strength to keep his feet planted in the slightly slippery, muddy bottom but he doubted that Ernest would do the same. On getting to the middle, the water level rose to his shoulder. He was lightly swimming this time, and they would definitely need the branch.

On getting to the other side, resting his bag on a nearby tree root and pulling off his outer jacket, he picked up the heavy branch and threw it across the water, being careful to let the heavier side stay with him.

Ernest gestured for her to go first, remembering the teachings of his mother on how to treat a woman. To him, Reba was a woman before she became a thief.

She reached the banks slowly. Putting one foot into the ravine, she grabbed the branch and started walking into the cool, fast-flowing water. She almost fell, cursing her small weight and earning a shout from Frederick for her to hold on to the branch for dear life.

It was Ernest's turn. He picked up the heavy sword and misjudged the way. He almost fell backwards but planted his feet firmly on the ground, remembering Frederick's words about using the sword: "The weight of a sword will cut you down if you are not firm like a rock."

Slowly, he entered the ravine. Reaching for the branch, he stepped into the fast-moving water, taking his time in the shallow end before venturing into the deeper part.

Reba scrunched up her face. "Anytime today," she said, bored of the current exchange.

They were losing daylight. Looking behind her into the forest, the unknown lay before the trio shrouded in mystery. A gasp caught in her throat. For a brief moment, she was sure she saw a pair of glowing eyes staring back at her. Fearful, she took a step back, nearly stepping into the ravine.

Her eyes went to Frederick, who looked back at her anxiety filling his eyes. She shook her head, brandishing what she had just seen. Chalking it up to the effects of the mosquito bites.

Ernest finally climbed up the shores of the ravine. The sun had nearly disappeared from the horizon. They made haste into the forest, searching for a suitable campsite to spend the night. They worked fast under the cover of the reddish hue of sunset. They found a small clearing surrounded by four large trees.

Quickly, they set up their camp with Ernest going off to find dried wood to serve as fuel for their campfire. Frederick lay down his sword and began pulling logs to serve as a bit of protection and pillows for when they would sleep.

After a few moments, Ernest came back cradling many dried twigs in his arms as he shivered slightly from the cold. Reba ran to him to help him with the wood, needing to get her blood moving as well.

Ernest arranged the twigs in a pyramid while Frederick battled with the flint in order to light it. After a few tries, they had fire and were being warmed by its heat.

The group feasted on some wet bread and slightly wet beef jerky, quenching their thirst from the water skins given to them by Pearlie. Frederick finished his meal, first getting up, picking up his sword in the process.

"I will take the first watch," he declared, leaving no room for argument.

A few hours later, Frederick sat atop the lowest branch of one of the trees facing south, his eyes staring around the camp and ensuring that if an animal would come close, it would be the gentle kind like rabbits and deer.

The only problem was that Frederick did not see any rabbits or deer. It was strange. He had been to this forest before and saw plenty of deer and curious rabbits many times. The only other explanation would have been that they were in wolf territory, which would explain the light yip he heard. The wolves would avoid fire—all you had to do was keep the fire burning all night long.

He climbed down softly from his perch to add more wood to the flames when Reba started convulsing violently. Her sounds jolted Ernest from his sleep, rushing to keep her arms and legs from flailing about.

"How is she so strong?" Ernest complained as he held her legs down. Frederick looked up at him, he had no answers to give. After a few grueling minutes, she stopped with the convulsions and her breath evened out.

"They are coming," she kept muttering as she opened her eyes.

"What is coming? What are they?" Ernest asked. He couldn't understand her words. Shaking her shoulders lightly, he helped her sit up.

"Nightmares," she whispered. "The nightmares are coming."

As if on cue, they heard a heavy howl coming from all directions. Ernest's ears were ringing and he screamed out in pain. Frederick, brandishing his sword, stooped into a combat position ready to defend his companions.

Reba was still stunned from her experience. All she could do was hug her knees to her chest and rock gently back and forth, shaking her head to repeat, "No!" over and over again.

Frederick picked up a pair of knives from his bag and handed it to a confused Ernest. He quickly barked out instructions to the inexperienced young man

"One to block and one to attack… repeat after me."

Ernest repeated the words and Frederick went on.

"Do you favor your right or your left?"

"My right," Ernest answered. He was visibly shaken, but they had to do this together.

"Block with your left, stab with your right. What did I say?" Ernest repeated his words.

He would take a crash course on how to handle short swords. The nightmares were closer now… he could hear their snarling breath as they ran, zipping through the wind.

The first one emerged from the darkness, bathing in the glow of the campfire. The creature before them bore no semblance of a normal wolf.

It stood on two feet—its fur the color of the darkest night. This wolf did not mind the flame, rather, it looked at it, chuckling at their pathetic excuse of a defense.

Another wolf emerged, and then another. Soon, they were surrounded by tall human-like wolves.

The wolves whispered instead of snapping their teeth at them.

"Why don't you close your eyes and take a nap? Don't you feel tired?" they whispered to the young knight.

Ernest had heard of them. They were called nightmares as Reba had said and their existence was to plague the realms of dreams. All he needed to do was stay awake, or else they would be in trouble.

"Frederick! Open your eyes, Frederick!" Ernest pushed.

Frederick frowned. Of course he was awake. He knew what they were and how fatal falling asleep would be. And of course, he wasn't asleep… he could see what was before him.

Ernest saw creatures made out of smoke and shadow itself. These creatures could not harm physical beings for they could only enter into his dreamscapes once he slept.

Ernest unsheathed one of the daggers and lightly pricked Frederick in his backside, warranting a shout from the young knight.

Frederick turned to look at the wolves before him and found they were different now, not the howling beasts he saw a few seconds earlier. They were made of shadow and smoke, just as Ernest had said.

Reba was standing now with a frown on her face. She had gotten over her fears a bit.

"Does this mean we will have to stay awake all night?" she asked in indignation and horror at the fact that she would lose sleep for these creatures. She never played with her sleep time.

Ernest returned the knives and sat by the fire, adding one piece, then two pieces of wood making the flames burn fresh.

"Yes," he said after the long pause. They would have to stay awake. He looked up from the flames, his eyes roaming over the nightmares that floated around.

"They will not do us much harm as long as we don't sleep."

And so, they spent the night awake. The only respite they had was that the morning would soon come. The sun rose with renewed hope as the group steadily made their way eastbound to the lands of the Whispering Woods hundreds of leagues ahead of them.

Exhaustion racked their bodies as they had stayed awake all through the night. Ernest read a scroll that showed him how to stay protected even while asleep. Dreaming was especially a liability that one must harness.

He had assumed that since he was the only one who could dream, the rest of the group would not be affected by creatures such as nightmares.

He explained that only a dreamer could see nightmares for what they were within the dreamscapes and without. They were otherwise invisible to the regular person.

He further explained that in order to protect yourself in dreams, you must build yourself something. It could be anything —a sword, a shield... you could even wish yourself a horse. You could imagine anything but only if you knew how it worked.

At least that's what he thought. He did not know much of the dreamscapes himself as he was no elite, so his knowledge was limited to the scrolls he found here and there and the whispers he heard. He taught them that the foundation of dreamscapes was just as solid as the foundation of reality, and sometimes, the foundations merged.

He explained that they were not like parallel lines for they would always cross their paths. He went on to say, "The more you know about the way the world works, the more you can craft an adequate defense for yourself within the dreamscapes. Many elites once used it to wage battles against each other. They would mount up defenses, build battle and siege engines, and lay waste to each other's dreamscapes, and it was proven that if a man died in his dreamscapes, he died in reality."

He further explained that because exploring and prospering in the dreamscapes was heavily based on what you knew and what you had access to. Which was why those with active imaginations and knowledge could do so. That, of course, was one of the reasons the elites deemed it fit to limit anyone who was not a high born from dreaming.

Dreaming was always the first step in accessing the dreamscapes. He explained that because many regular people had hope, the hope would translate into imagination, that imagination could work well once such a person entered the dreamscapes. All of that did not mean just anyone could dream. The ability seemed to be exhibited by a few, although he didn't know why.

Hearing that amplified the sense of dread his companions felt. "But how come we are dreaming? We are not dreamers," Frederick said. Ernest gazed ahead of them as they walked eastward. He did not know the answer to that question—he could only speculate.

Reba, lifting her legs over a fallen log, commented, "Maybe it's because we are outside of Dream Haven."

There was a rumor in the underground that said the dreams were regulated because the elites used hidden powers in the dreamscapes to grow stronger and extend their influence across the continent. They say that there were hidden treasures within the dreamscapes and that they had used magic to limit as many people as possible within the city from ever dreaming. Ernest thought that perhaps it would make sense that everybody would dream once they were out of Dream Haven.

That only made him want to fix all the problems with Dream Haven. His heart was heavy when he remembered his life and how everything was ruined by the elite of Dream Haven. "Dreams should not be regulated. They shouldn't be reserved for a few", he said with anger.

That night, they were attacked in their sleep by nightmares. This time, they were ready. Or so they thought. Before them was the largest nightmare wolf they had seen. It stood to almost 10 feet and looked like many smaller ones merged.

Frederick, taking the lead in the fight, snapped the remaining two out of their momentary daze with a call to action. "Just like we've practiced, guys!"

CHAPTER 6

BONDS BEYOND BLOOD

Reba took the rear, firing arrows from her crossbow, alternating it with her throwing knives. Frederick and Ernest took turns in striking the beast. Together, they had dealt much damage and the beast fell to the floor.

A few moments later, while the group caught their breath, the nightmare wolf stood up, fully healed. The group shared a look of surprise and fear. "Here we go again," Frederick said as he raised his sword.

This time, they did not stop their attacks even when the beast fell. They kept hitting it until it dissolved into smoke, signaling its death. With a heave and a sigh, the group fell in exhaustion. They lay on the soft grass for a while before Frederick urged them to get up.

Reba refused, and so did Ernest. In the end, they had to settle for sitting and resting their backs against each other.

When Ernest opened his eyes, it was morning. He shook his companions awake. Reba opened heavy eyes at him. "Ten more minutes. Please. I just fell into a deep sleep," she mumbled. He couldn't help but grant her the request.

Frederick, however, was fully awake and stretching with a

groan. He took a seat beside Reba's sleeping form. He and Ernest spoke quietly about the journey. Ernest complained that he wasn't very sure their supplies would last them another week or two.

"We just need to find water," Frederick said knowingly.

Ernest looked at him squarely and asked if he had ever been outside Dream Haven, to which the knight affirmed. Frederick expressed that he wasn't sure why they dreamt. He explained that when he journeyed to the knight's citadel in the snowy wilderness, he did not dream.

"Do you think it's because of me?" Ernest asked.

"Maybe... a lot of things happen because of you. The prophecy is mostly about you."

Ernest looked at Reba's sleeping form. Ten minutes had passed but he made no move to wake her up. His thoughts staying on what the knight said. It made sense. He knew it was because of him. For that, he would take responsibility for their safety within the dreamscapes. His conscience would allow nothing less.

Frederick led them through the dense forest for another day until the vegetation started to thin. Reba expressed her joy at being able to see the sun, earning a laugh from them. Frederick informed them that they would soon break free of the forest.

True to his word, they breached the forest the following evening.

The group had finally breached the wall of trees separating them from the forest and the gentle rolling hills that lay before them. At a distance, they spotted a cluster of buildings. The group hurried over a small hill with the sun almost down as they made their way swiftly in order to set up for the night.

On getting there, they observed that it was once a small village, although abandoned for many years now as most of the buildings had turned to rubble. Some were even nothing more than empty lots, but surprisingly, they had much wood to burn as fuel for their comfort fire.

Agreeing amongst themselves, they would make a quick

exploration of the historic site before them, then meet back at the largest clearing in the shape of a whole, which Frederick speculated to be the village hall. So, off they went to explore the ruins and gather wood in the process.

Ernest traced his steps back to where they came from, heading to the mouth of the village. He walked to the first house—at least what was left of it—and found a broken table. It had a fireplace and two inner rooms. He suspected a family lived there. He remembered his small family, his heart aching with the memories.

He grabbed the table legs, testing the dryness, and judging them to be dry, he walked out of the ruined building, his eyes silently searching for his companions. He felt relieved when he saw Frederick's golden head towards the south end of the village.

He knew he could not really find Reba, but he was sure she would be fine. The thief was more resourceful than the two of them combined.

He continued his exploration of the ruins in peace, observing the various marks on the building, testing to see if they were left by beasts or just the natural wear and tear and erosion of the buildings.

Checking for more of these signs and picking up wood along the way, he concluded that they were safe from nightmares and other wild beasts. Reba cursed the elite bastards within Dream Haven. She felt it was wrong of them to limit access into the dreamscapes because of the treasures that lay with it.

Of course, treasures were her motivation, but the question was... how would she access the treasures now?

Distance within the dreamscapes was the same as the distance within physical reality, so traveling through dreamscapes was just like traveling through reality. Unless, of course, she imagined she would turn herself into a bird and fly to the top of the great cliffs of dreamscapes.

She had grown rather fond of the planes for the remaining shadows since there was no sun. The sky was a permanent color of different shades of purple and blue. The source of light seemed to be coming from nowhere and everywhere at the same time.

The dreamscapes were not dark, neither were they bright.

She thought about how quickly she would build herself a mansion within the dreamscapes before they returned to Dream Haven. She learned that wealth was measured in what you have in the dreamscapes and how you could translate it into physical attributes—that was the problem… in order to exchange the items or the energy you found or the achievements within the dreamscapes, you needed magic. Magic was beyond a common person like her.

Only the highborn and the elites could afford to obtain the magic. She filled her lungs with air, sensing serenity and peace. She picked up a couple of more pieces of wood and turned to their agreed meeting place.

Frederick barely explored the ghost village. He did not like the thought of picking up valuables and leaving the home that you had built. He found it strange to run from a fight as one of the tenets of being a knight was to stand and face an adversary as a worthy foe.

He, of course, understood that the village people were nothing more than gentle folk and would run at the sign of trouble, so he did not fault them for leaving their homes behind. Frederick returned to the agreed campsite and decided to set up.

The soft, almost inaudible footsteps of the thief approached the place as he had just finished making the fire pit. He dug the floor a few inches deep and arranged stones in a circle to keep the flames from spreading. The thief laid her bounty beside him, giving him a nod of acknowledgement as she sat down to unravel the contents of her bag. When she was done with that, she moved on to unwrapping her crossbow and freeing her waist of the daggers.

Not long after, a soft flicker of a flame bloomed just as Ernest walked into the campsite. He smiled at his companions as he dropped his own bounty, easily three times the size of the one collected by Reba. He dropped the twin daggers given to him by Frederick on the ground beside him, rubbed his hands together, and placed them in front of the flickering flames.

He looked up from the flames and met both of their eyes. Having their attention, he reached into his pocket and pulled out what appeared to be a small scroll, which did not contain much—it was just a letter left behind by mistake.

The letter was written to somebody's cousin telling them of how they had to leave in a rush because they could not stand the relentless onslaught of the nightmares. And so, in a last effort, the village's inhabitants fled. As Ernest finished reading the letter, tears welled up in his eyes, remembering his mother's unjust death.

He cleaned his eyes and looked at the flame once more. His next words were slow and deliberate, "I barely know either of you and we've spent gods know how long on this journey. I will tell you something about myself if you tell me something about you. I think we should learn to trust each other if we are to survive."

The two remained silent as approval rang in the air. Ernest opened up about his mother's death and about the event that led up to it. He emphasized how much he felt like it was his fault because he could not keep his excitement to himself.

He regretted greatly how he could not see beyond his nose when it came to things that excited him as a child... the way he would go about spreading the news to everyone even when his mother told him not to. He finished the story with heart-wrenching sobs. Frederick handed him the skin of water.

Ernest accepted it. Frederick looked up from the flames. It was his turn now and he bit his lip.

"I'm bored of an immoral union between an elite and a commoner." He informed them of how his father's family did not wish to accept him initially, but that they had no choice after his mother's untimely death when he was two winters old. Because his father's family could not accept him as their son, they decided to put him through the ways of being a knight.

Knights did not marry, so he would not pass on the family name. Instead, he would live his life forever in servitude to the family he served. He went on to describe his stepbrother as being a narcissist and self-entitled brat who chose every possible way to make his life a living hell.

Upon joining the knight academy when he was 13 winters old, his mind was forged into the unbreakable chalice of knighthood until it was time for their first journey. For part of being a knight was to venture out in a group and then alone, beyond everything you knew.

A journey of self-discovery, they called it. It was a journey that ended up with all three of his companions dead. He ran from the danger ahead of him, he recalled with tears running down his face. Frederick finished his tale with losing his companions, knowing that he was never knighted because he did not fulfill his code of honor to his friends.

In his heart, he felt it would have been better for him to die and then come back, and the shame of being knighted.

Reba took a deep breath. Everybody was telling stories and trying to get closer. Her life was simple, which she was grateful for. She peered at the faces before her, illuminated by the gentle glow of the fire.

She watched their faces for signs of betrayal but found none. She searched their eyes, gazing into the depths of their souls to find treachery and all the vices that made men evil, and all she saw was just broken and damaged people, hurt by those who were supposed to love them.

Somewhere in her heart, she yearned to comfort them. But all she could offer was her own story. She looked back down into the fire, the hypnotizing dance almost drawing her in.

She began with how she had no parents. All she remembered was her teacher. The man carried her on his shoulders. He clothed her, fed her, and taught her everything she knew about being a swift and nimble thief who loved the shadows. She remembered when he gifted her the crossbow. He had disappeared for two weeks, only to return with the weapon slung across his back.

She had danced about the small cottage, pleading with him to teach her how to fire true.

The dark-skinned man told her that her only strength was in herself, and her weakness was in trusting others. According to him, if a man had not proven himself time and time again, others could trust him, but she should not care even if the man lay his life down, she would still not trust him. And for all her life, she believed that to be true. She would never trust even if it killed her. It was the only way to survive the life she had lived and she had no regrets.

If not for this lesson, she would have fallen prey to many who wished her harm. She had avoided many near-death experiences because she learned to walk alone. Her teacher—unfortunately, her only family—met his end trusting his only living brother.

His brother had lured him, pleading with him that they would steal an orb from within the coffers of some great family and how they would split the proceeds equally. She wanted a stake in the operation so she could prove herself to her teacher, but he refused vehemently, telling her she was not ready to take on work like that. "Besides, you've already proven yourself to me many times. You're simply not ready for this one." He had told her he would be gone for four days at the latest.

She waited and waited and waited for two weeks. One day, she got tired of waiting and ventured away from their small cottage. She went into the bustling streets beneath the slums and strolled helplessly searching for her teacher. She found him. Or rather, she found his head on a spike with a plank that had an inscription made on it: "A thief caught in the act." Luckily, he taught her to read.

She cleared her throat before continuing her story whilst

fighting the tears that threatened to burst out of the dams of her eyes.

She had never told this story to anyone and had never cried before anyone except her teacher. She would honor him with that. She glossed over a life after his death. About how she lived having no choice but to resort to stealing and selling her services out as a mercenary.

It was hard to establish herself as that for she was a young girl. Not many people were willing to entrust their safety in the hands of a small woman. But she fought, and soon, she claimed a piece of the city as her territory, having her own small crew of thieves that did her bidding, pickpocketing and collecting information.

Dreams were expensive only for the nobility and the highborn, but information was expensive amongst common folk like her. Ernest handed her the water skin.

She did not want their comfort, but Ernest's eyes shone with understanding and lack of judgment, he was genuine and so was Frederick. The dams she kept bottled up inside cracked for the first time— the salty waters leaking through her eyes as she took the skin from Ernest's hands. Perhaps she could try trusting these two. Perhaps she could not worry about stealing to survive. They had saved each other multiple times on the journey.

She looked at Ernest and Frederick with tears running down her face. She had decided she would trust them. She would follow them.

Ernest smiled as she took the water skin from him.

They chatted away about small things into the night. Their laughter sounded until the wee hours of the morning when they finally slept.

The group decided to stay at the village for a few more days. Before them was a great snowy wilderness called the Icy Peaks. Frederick explained that the peaks were home to the knight's citadel where young knights in training would journey to. Upon reaching the citadel, they would bathe in icy water, train until they dropped and, most importantly, they'd journey to the innermost parts of the wilderness to fight together. The idea was that a knight must learn to protect members of his company. It was believed that they would build character and valor when they faced danger together.

Frederick paused, remembering the faces of those he left.

"You know what? I doubt if you two would ever survive the journey to the citadel. It's cold—very cold. You'll suffer frostbite and frozen lungs before we get there," the knight said while laughing.

Their plan was to refill their supplies and, hopefully, learn more about the dreamscapes. They learned that the library of the citadels contained many texts on all manner of topics and that the keeper of the citadel, being a dwarf, could repair their weapons.

The surprise on Reba's face was apparent when the word "dwarf" left Frederick. It was known that many species roamed the earth besides humans. Faeries, dryads, imps, and elves shared the world with them. Frederick explained that because of something that happened centuries ago, the others did not relate with humans. They had mostly cut off communication with them. He spoke of how great archers the elves were. How the fairies were linked to the gods and goddesses. The dryads, guardians of truth, the dwarves in their caverns were masters of craft.

According to him, a great war occurred, causing the races to band together to stop the great terror. He didn't know the intricacies, but he assumed that the knowledge was long since lost.

"Dwarves were a secretive bunch. Balin is the only one I've seen. I heard he was banished by his kin for loving a human," Frederick explained to them. "I'm telling you this because I don't want you to be surprised when you see him. Act natural."

Over the next few days, the temperature dropped as they approached the peaks. Ernest was already sneezing and Reba was rubbing her palms together to keep warmth.

In order to keep his friends warm, Frederick made them train until they dripped with sweat. Ernest especially, being thin, needed more strength.

He would even make them run some parts of the journey until they dropped in exhaustion. Twice, they had to make camp out of this.

Frederick expected that Ernest and Reba would complain. He was glad they didn't. They knew the stakes of the quest and he was pleased he didn't have to explain it to them.

The group fought more hulking nightmare wolves in the dreamscapes. They were, however, better at it. They would spend less than 30 minutes finishing one off as opposed to the over one hour they spent when they encountered the first one.

Ernest was most excited about his progress with the daggers. He moved quickly and surely. Sometimes, he surprised himself when he'd become one with shadows, blending into the environment. He was like an assassin as they began the climb to the Icy Peaks.

CHAPTER 7

ECHOES OF HONOR

The group continued their journey to the east. Frederick's mood seemed to get worse the more they journeyed as he had mentioned that the tragedy of his friends happened somewhere in the east.

Ernest gazed at the young knight, wishing to offer comfort as they had shared before. However, they needed to rush. They were losing daylight quickly and there was no place they could use as a camp nearby.

It would seem that the group would have to journey through the night if they wished to be safe. The temperature dropped to the point where their breaths came out as mist. Frederick was the only one who had experienced a cold like this. Shivers racked his group members as he set down his bags and sword.

He had no blanket but he gave them his extra clothes—a large jacket and shirt for each of them. Quickly, they both shrugged off their blankets and put on Frederick's large clothes. They then picked up their blankets and resumed their journey with Frederick at the helm.

For two days, the group did not see anything until they spotted a lonely tower on top of a jagged peak. The site of his old knight citadel brought tears to his eyes as Frederick took a small step forward. He wanted to go back.

He felt the soft yet firm hand of Ernest on his shoulder. Raising his eyes to meet his gaze, Frederick found comfort and resolve. With newfound determination, he led them to the tower.

The group had arrived at the great hulking gates of the tower. It was larger up close. Frederick stepped forward and knocked on the wooden doors with all his might. The gate opened a few seconds later, revealing a dwarf with an apron about his waist.

The dwarf, Bailing, recognizing the young man before him, then scowled and stepped aside. It was dishonorable to turn away those seeking peace and warmth. That was the citadel's number one rule.

The group walked into the large courtyard. The simple gray stone architecture was nothing spectacular, but the stones spoke of age and time. They would lay on top of each other for another millennia.

The dwarf led them to the dining hall, which was filled with basic long tables and a long bench. The utilitarianism of the designer was apparent even in its furniture. He gestured for them to pick a seat while mumbling to himself about telling her to show them to their rooms.

Reba and Ernest visibly exhaled and relaxed into the wooden bench. It was much softer than sleeping on the floor. Their backsides and feet thanked them.

Frederick's somber mood had returned. He must have found something fascinating on the boring- looking table. His gaze was solely focused on the dark wood.

A woman wearing a basic frock with a washed-out apron stepped out of the back room, speaking at the top of her lungs, "How could he not tell me we had visitors? For so long, I've missed the sight of people—" She paused upon seeing Frederick.

"Oh, my sweet child," she said. "I have missed you!" She stretched out her hands, offering a comforting embrace. Frederick laid his head on her large bosom, inhaling the scent of spices and herbs. He cried once again, with sobs and soft wails rocking his large body.

The dwarf lingered at the doorway to what must have been the kitchen. His eyes roamed over the two strained travelers who followed Frederick.

For the first time in over three months, the group ate a hot meal consisting of freshly baked bread and potato and pork stew. The taste of a home-cooked meal brought tears to their eyes as they had forgotten what love tasted like.

The dwarf showed them to their rooms. The boys would share one, and the small lady would have one to herself. Reba wanted to ask if she could get a bath. Her words dying in her throat as she saw a wooden bath filled with hot water.

Ernest plopped on the large bed. He had never been in a room this large nor had he seen a bath so big. Frederick chuckled as he took off his clothes, getting ready to dip himself in the wooden bath.

Ernest looked up at the ceiling, feeling the need to speak. "It was here, wasn't it?" he said to the ceiling. Frederick's silence gave him the answer he needed.

Just as he had said, he lost his friends fighting a nightmare not far from this citadel. Ernest, wanting no more, sat up on the bed so he could face the man he called his new friend.

"Ever since we started climbing the steep rocks, you have been distant and cold. Is it something you would like to talk about?" he asked.

Frederick kept silent for a moment. "It's hard being here. Everywhere I look, I think about the horrifying way they died. I remember the fear in their eyes. Peter looked at me, his eyes pleading with me to pull his shattered body away to safety. But I just stood… frozen. Watching my friends get torn apart. I lost my honor that day. And I do not know if I can ever get it back," he said with a heavy heart.

Ernest was ignorant of the ways and codes of knights. All he could do was offer his sympathy. He deduced that, for a knight, losing his honor was the same as losing an arm or leg.

Ernest got up from his soft seat, walking to the window and staring out into the snowy wilderness before him. According to the map, after the wilderness, they would head northbound to find the Whispering Woods.

"If perhaps you found your honor, do you think you could lead us to the Whispering Woods?" he asked his friend, hoping to hear his voice.

Frederick cupped his hands, lifting water to his face. He gazed at his reflection, clearing his mind just a bit.

"Once a knight loses his honor, he cannot gain it back. But yes, I can lead you to the Whispering Woods and then beyond. But I don't know if I can be the man you want me to be," he said bitterly.

Reba soaked herself until her skin turned pink and her fingers and toes wrinkled. 'It has been so long,' she thought to herself as she pulled her linen shirt over her head.

Her mind reached out to Frederick, remembering his demeanor when they were close to the citadel. She promised herself to have a quick talk with him. He was normally centered, so it was hard to watch him break down.

She often imagined him like a strong tower—a beacon of hope, a protector. It was strange seeing the man crumble into a sopping mess before the plump woman.

Reba had learned that her name was Melissa. And the dwarf was Balin.

She opened her door, peering from right to left until she came out and closed it behind her softly.

She walked over to Ernest and Frederick's room, knocking on the door, hoping they were decent. Ernest opened the door clad in a clean white shirt, his cheeks were rosy and his hair was wet.

Her eyes moved to look for Frederick, found sitting on the bed with his head cast down. She walked into the room, determined to talk to him. She bent down in front of him so she could catch his eyes.

"Do you recall the time you threw me the branch? How about the multiple times you saved our lives on the way to this citadel? If that is not honor, then please explain to me that I am a thief after all and I did not know what honor is."

He looked at her, about to speak, when there was a harsh knock on the door. A man poked his head into the room, saying, "We need your help."

The group hurried down the stairs of the keep to find Melissa pacing the floors. Her dwarfish husband clasped her hands, calming her down.

She looked up. "Nightmares are outside. Not the wolves." Tears welled up in her eyes. "The minotaur."

'It was a minotaur that killed his friends,' Reba thought to herself. Frederick was no longer a knight in training. He was now a man.

She placed her hand on his shoulder, reassuring him that he was not alone.

Together, they walked out of the citadel's gates. Brandishing their weapons, they faced the great beast before them.

They returned with a renewed sense of hope. Their hearts lit anew. Frederick underwent the biggest transformation among the three.

He had found his honor. The code was strong in his heart. He was ready to lead his companions on the treacherous journey to the sword. Reba smiled at him.

"I knew you'd find it," she remarked. Ernest laughed and then grimaced as the movement caused a strain on his injured ribs.

"Let's just go inside and wash off this blood and grime, please," he said with a soft voice.

CHAPTER 8

WAKING NIGHTMARES

It was a dark and stormy night, and the group was seeking shelter from the raging storm. They had been lost in the woods for hours and were starting to lose hope as the storm grew angrier by the second.

The group were caught out in the full force of the storm. The wind whipped around them, howling like a beast, and the rain soaked through their clothes, chilling them to the bone.

The noise of thunder and lightning crashed overhead, and the ground beneath their feet was sodden and muddy. They had no choice but to seek shelter, their hearts pounding with fear as the storm raged around them.

As the rain poured down and the wind howled, they stumbled upon a small, dilapidated cottage, and they all ran towards it like it was a trophy. Left with no choice as it was the only shelter they could find, they knocked on the door, hoping for a place to stay.

"You think they'll come out?" Frederick asked against gritted teeth, shivering from the cold. His rain- soaked clothes clinging to his skin.

"They wouldn't let poor humans like us die in the cold, would they?" Ernest replied. "Not if they aren't humans," Reba chuckled dryly.

Surprisingly, the door creaked open and they were greeted by a tall, hooded figure. They could not see the figure's face, but they knew they had found something more than just shelter.

They had stumbled into the cottage like a group of hungry mice and stood at the door in uniform.

The sorcerer was a tall and imposing figure, clad in the blackest color robe they'd ever seen. They could feel the sorcerer's presence—a sense of power and authority that was both comforting and unsettling.

As they stepped into the cottage, the air was thick with the smell of incense and spices, and the room was filled with books, scrolls, and other mysterious objects.

The cottage was a strange and otherworldly place, filled with objects and artifacts that seemed out of place in the natural world.

The walls were lined with shelves of books, their spines embossed with strange symbols and writing. Scrolls were piled high in corners, and vials of mysterious liquids and powders lined the tables. An odd-looking telescope was positioned in front of a window, pointing towards the night sky. Candles flickered in every corner, casting eerie shadows on the walls. And the floor was covered with strange symbols and patterns etched into the wood. It was a place that was both alien and yet strangely beautiful.

The sorcerer gestured for them to sit, and they did so without uttering a word, their hearts pounding in their chests. The man looked at them without saying a word, and they felt as if they were being examined, their very souls laid bare.

There was a small fireplace in the center of the room. The man gestured towards the fire, and they all felt the warmth of the flames, driving away the chill of the stormy night.

Everything felt so strange as the man offered them tea, still without saying a word to them, and they accepted gratefully.

As they sipped the herbal brew, they felt their minds begin to clear, their thoughts sharpening.

"You've come a long way," the man finally spoke in a low voice. "Where are you going?" he asked. "We're treasure hunting," Frederick said, but Ernest struck him lightly on the elbow, interrupting him.

"You see, we are just travelers. We're in search of a nice place to live, start a business and… you know, probably start a family too," Ernest said, and the rest of the group members nodded in affirmation.

"Really?" the man asked, unconvinced, but didn't say any more as he gave them their space.

The group huddled in the cottage, the storm raging outside. The sky was dark and overcast, the thunder rumbling like a great beast in the distance. Inside, the fire crackled in the hearth, casting flickering shadows on the walls. Each of the trio was dressed in travel-worn clothes, their cloaks and boots caked with mud and rainwater. Their hair was windswept and their eyes were tired, but their spirits were lifted by the warmth of the fire and the soothing taste of the stranger's tea.

Once again, the man began to indulge them in a conversation and they found him to be great company. They all spoke of the mysteries of the universe, of the hidden truths of the world that lay beyond the grasp of the ordinary senses. As they spoke, the group felt a sense of wonder and awe as if they were being transported to another realm. It was a world of boundless knowledge and they felt engrossed by the old man's display of wisdom and age.

Just moments ago, they were wrestling with the cold outside, but now, as they sat by the fire, the storm felt distant. It was as if it belonged to another world.

The group stood in a circle, holding hands, their faces lit by the flickering light of the fire. The night was dark and still, and they could feel the energy in the air crackling with tension.

Suddenly, a shadowy figure emerged from the darkness, its features obscured by the night.

Reba rushed to Ernest and stood by his side while Frederick drew his sword. "What's that?" Reba asked the old man, but he only shrugged.

"I have no idea," he replied.

The figure was obscure. It began to speak, its voice low and menacing, and the group could feel the hairs on the back of their necks stand on end.

Then the old man began to laugh as the figure slowly disappeared into oblivion. "What in god's name was that?" Ernest asked, but the old man gave no reply.

Ernest, Reba, and Frederick were bound together by a shared love of adventure and a desire to push the boundaries of what was possible. But as they stood in the circle, facing the old man whose name they didn't know, their bonds were put to the test.

"Tell me about your fears, each of you," the old man asked.

"So you can use it against us?" Reba asked, looking really pissed. "We're telling you nothing," Frederick said.

The old man walked back and forth in the room, grumbling words as he adjusted himself into a seat and faced them with keen interest.

"What?" Ernest asked, feeling the old man's stare begin to burn a hole in his chest. "If you won't talk, I'll make you," the man said.

Suddenly, they felt their heads begin to twirl and things flew to the ground, making crazy noises. They all covered their ears with their palms as they began feeling dizzy and sick. They were caught in a web of illusion.

Reba's illusions took the form of her greatest fear—a world where she was old and poor. She saw herself as an old woman, alone and forgotten, living a life of drudgery and despair.

Ernest's illusions showed him the death of his closest friends, one by one, until he was the last one standing. Frederick's illusions showed him a future where he was trapped in an endless cycle of poverty and abuse, unable to escape his circumstances.

For Reba, her illusions were the most poignant as they reflected her deepest fears. In the illusion, she was an old woman, living alone in a small, rundown cottage. The years had taken their toll on her, and she was frail and weak. She was surrounded by dusty books and fading memories, and she spent her days staring into the fire, lost in thought. The world had moved on without her, and she felt like a relic

of the past with no place in the future. It was a terrifying and lonely existence, and Reba couldn't shake the feeling that this was her fate.

"No!" she screamed.

This was not the future Reba was looking forward to, so she fought against the illusion, and in doing so, she found the strength to face her fears. She knew that she needed to keep fighting for the future she wanted, no matter what.

For Ernest, his illusions were the most tragic. In them, he watched his only family over and over again until his coarse screams echoed for all time. He watched as the new family he had found in Frederick and Reba broke as their deaths were played to him in a never-ending vision. He was the last one left. He saw himself as a lonely and broken man, unable to find meaning or purpose in a world without the people he loved. It was a bleak and desolate future, and Ernest felt a deep sense of loss and despair. A soulful groan escaped his throat.

He saw himself walking down the road at night, feeling a sense of loneliness and isolation. All around him, he saw people walking hand in hand, their faces lit up with love and companionship. But he was alone, without the people he cared about. He felt like an outsider, a stranger in a world full of happy couples.

As he passed each couple, he wondered what it would be like to have someone to share his life with, someone to walk hand in hand with down the street. He felt a pang of sadness, and every pound of hope was lost in him. But in facing his fears, he found the strength to carry on. He realized that even if he lost the people he loved, he still needed to live his life to the fullest. And in doing so, he could honor their memory and keep their spirit alive.

Frederick's illusions were the most surreal. He found himself in a world where everything was wrong and distorted—where nothing made sense. People and objects were shifting and changing, and he felt like he was losing his grip on reality.

"Hold me!" he yelled to no one in particular. He couldn't hear anything, and he had no idea where he was anymore as everything was just disjointed.

The only voice he heard was that of the old man mocking and also daring him to find his way.

It was a frightening and disorienting experience, but in the end, Frederick found the courage to face the chaos. He realized that even in the midst of uncertainty and confusion, he needed to find the strength to believe in himself and his own intuition.

No matter how strange or unsettling things became, he knew that he could find his way through it. And as he emerged from the illusions, he felt a renewed sense of self-confidence and strength. He knew that no matter what challenges lay ahead, he could face them head-on.

All three of them had faced their fears, and in doing so, they were changed forever. They found a new strength and resilience that would carry them through the darkest of times.

Their illusions were powerful and frightening, but the group refused to break their hold on each other's hands. They faced their fears together, knowing that they would emerge stronger if they could survive the experience.

And when the illusions faded away, they found themselves standing together, their bonds stronger than ever before. But the scars of their experience were evident, and they knew that they would never be the same again. But in that moment, they knew that they were ready to face whatever came next.

As each member felt the grip of the illusion loosen, and they slumped to the ground feeling tired and wasted, the old man strolled towards them and crouched beside them.

"Stay away from us!" Frederick commanded the old sorcerer both out of fear and anger.

"How was your experience?" he asked, beaming with joy as a loud and throaty chuckle escaped his throat like a goat's bleat.

"Tell me you had nothing to do with that?" Reba asked.

"Oh, I wish I could say that, but I can't. You all know that was me, and I was only trying to help you fight your deepest fears and find your strength," the old sorcerer replied, still crouching beside the trio.

"What did you gain from that?" Ernest asked.

"I didn't, but you did," the old sorcerer replied. "You stood your ground and fought neck to neck against your fears, and that's victory. You may hate me for it, but I could care less. I've helped you see the strength that lies in being fearless."

The man then walked to the window and looked outside. It was still dark and gloomy, but the rain had subsided and so had the storm.

"You can leave now, the storm is over," he announced.

The group stood up and stared out the window. They may be pissed off with the man for invading them without permission, but there was no way they were stepping out into the dark and cold of the night.

"Can we stay the night here?" Ernest asked, suddenly finding strength in his ability to lead and speak up for his team.

"Looks like you've found your voice," the old sorcerer said and chuckled lightly. "Of course you can stay. There's no way I was going to send you off in the middle of the night," he finished.

"Can I have a warm bath too?" Reba asked, suddenly sniffing her clothes and making a face like she'd kissed a frog.

"Anything for the lady," the old sorcerer said and gestured towards a darker room.

Reba's eyes shifted from the dark room to the old sorcerer and back to her teammates. "That?" she asked.

"Yes, that," the old sorcerer repeated. "But it's dark over there?" she queried. "Believe in yourself," the old sorcerer said.

Reba shook her head in disbelief but began whooshing towards the door. As she neared the threshold of the door, the candles flickered and there were lights shining everywhere in the bathroom.

The bathroom looked as mysterious and magical as the old sorcerer. It was filled with potions and strange contraptions. The walls were lined with shelves of jars and bottles, each filled with mysterious ingredients. The floor was tiled with intricate patterns, and the mirror was adorned with runes and symbols. A cauldron bubbled over the sink, and a broomstick leaned against the wall.

"Quite odd," Reba found herself saying as her hand fondled with the crystal ball that sat on a pedestal, its surface shimmering with light. Everything was strangely clean and sparkling, yet like the old man when they first entered his cottage, there was an air of mystery and magic about the room.

Reba found a vial that contained soap, which she used on her body. It gave off a sweet flowery scent like lavender and rose.

When she came out of the bathroom, she felt clean, and for the first time in a long time, she found that bath really soothing, reminding her of their time at the knight's citadel.

Ernest and Frederick took their turns right after Reba, and soon, the group were squeaky clean as they gathered around the fire again, staring at the old sorcerer as he slept peacefully in his old seat.

The sun rose over the horizon, its golden light spilled across the rolling hills that surrounded the cottage. Dew glistened on the grass and birdsong filled the air. The trees swayed gently in the morning breeze, their leaves rustling softly.

The cottage itself was nestled among the trees, its stone walls gleaming in the sunlight. Smoke curled up from the chimney, and the smell of freshly baked bread wafted through the air. All was peaceful and serene—a perfect start to a new day. And yet, there was a sense of magic in the air, a feeling of mystery. Ernest jerked awake and relaxed again after he looked around and felt safe where he was.

With the smell of freshly baked bread, and the morning progressing, the old sorcerer began to stir. He walked to the kitchen, where a pot of steaming tea awaited him. He poured himself a cup and sat at the table, gazing out the window at the tranquil landscape beyond. He took a sip of his tea and a contented smile crossed his face.

Reba had prepared breakfast and laid it on his rickety-looking dining table, and the old sorcerer sat to eat bread with the team as they talked about the night and their trip.

As the old sorcerer watched the world awaken, he knew that this was a perfect day to work on his spells and enchantments. He felt a sense of peace and calm, ready to face whatever the day would bring.

"What will you be doing today?" Reba asked the old sorcerer as she helped him clear the table and came to stand by her teammates.

"Minding my business, just like you," the old man answered with a laugh, and the trio made their way out the door, grateful for the shelter and for breakfast.

"Really minding your business." Ernest laughed, and they waved goodbye to the old sorcerer and waltzed off.

"That was a crazy experience we had back there at the cottage," Ernest said after they'd walked a distance.

"You know, I never quite doubted your strength," Frederick said to Ernest after he'd told the group what he'd been confronted with.

"Nor did I," Reba concurred.

"Why didn't you two ever tell me that?" he asked.

"Not that it would have changed how you feel about yourself," Frederick said. "I'm sure it does now," Ernest replied, walking away.

"I'm sure it does," Reba repeated, watching Ernest throttle down the plain and running to catch up.

As they walked away from the circle, each one of them felt a new sense of purpose and determination.

They knew they had been tested and that they had overcome a challenge that would make them stronger. They had faced their greatest fears, and in doing so, they emerged victorious. They were ready to face whatever came next with courage and conviction.

The experience had left its mark on them, but they were determined to make it a mark of strength and resilience. They would carry the scars of their illusions, but they would wear them with pride, knowing that they had overcome the impossible.

If there was anything else Ernest discovered from the illusion, it was that he was stronger than he looked and he would never let a horrible experience tear him up again. He would grow stronger.

CHAPTER 9

THE MERCHANT'S SECRET

As the trio spiraled through the woods, the early afternoon weather set in like a dream. The air was cool and crisp, with the scent of pine needles and damp earth. The sunlight streamed through the leaves, creating dappled patterns on the ground. A light mist hung in the air, making the trees seem to shimmer and sway.

The group kept moving as they sensed a feeling of peace and serenity. It was as if they had left the ordinary world behind. As they continued on their journey, the woods grew darker and the air became more still. There was a feeling of expectancy as if something was about to happen, but each time they neared the end of the road, another road seemed to resurrect.

"What the heck!? Are you certain we haven't missed a track?" Frederick asked, growing impatient. "Have we gotten there yet?" Reba asked, and Ernest was getting weary of their questions.

"Maybe one of you should hold the map and lead us through," Ernest said when he couldn't hold his anger anymore.

Everyone fell silent, each trying to curb their anger and frustration at their misfortune.

As the team trudged along the road, they heard a faint sound in the distance. It was a low, mournful howl like a wolf's cry.

The sound sent a chill down their spines, and they began to walk faster, their hearts pounding. Suddenly, they heard another sound, a rustling in the undergrowth. They froze, their eyes wide with fear, but the noise died down and they made a mad dash away from the scene.

"That had to be the worst nightmare in daylight," Frederick said. "You're right," Ernest replied.

"But we need to keep going, gentlemen," Reba said and hunched them all up. They started on their tracks again.

For a while, the team members traveled in silence with no one uttering a word.

The road the team traveled through was lined with overgrown hedges and gnarled trees, their branches reaching out like claws. The sky was beginning to turn gray and foreboding and the wind was now howling through the trees. The road was cracked and potholed, and the air was heavy with the scent of damp earth. The further the team walked, the more isolated they felt.

The road seemed to go on forever, twisting and turning through the dark, shadowy woods. The sense of foreboding only grew stronger, and the team began to wonder if they had made a terrible mistake in following Pearlie's map.

After what seemed like forever, Ernest glanced at the map and it seemed to be leading them down a winding path, through the woods and into a clearing.

"I think we've found a clue," he announced.

"Quite different from the trail we've been following all along?" Reba asked.

So, the team weaved through the woods and into the Midlands. There, they found themselves standing in front of a small, ramshackle cottage. The door was hanging off its hinges, and the windows were covered in cobwebs. The air was thick with a sense of foreboding. And yet, there was no sign of the sword.

"This isn't one of those jokes, is it?" Reba belched, visibly pissed but trying to hold it in as she did her fears.

"You mean like that of the old sorcerer? I hope not," Frederick answered.

The trio exchanged nervous glances and then knocked on the door. It creaked open slowly, revealing a darkened interior. And then, a voice spoke, low and raspy. "What do you want?"

"We know that Pearlie is in there," Ernest started. "We want answers," he continued, his voice trembling slightly. "We want to know why you gave us this map. We want to know what your true intentions are." There was a long silence, broken only by the sound of a crackling fire.

Finally, a figure emerged from the shadows, her face obscured by a hooded cloak. "I had my reasons," she said, her voice barely audible. "I have nothing more to say to you," she said and was about to shut the door when Reba held her by the cloak, Frederick kicked the door open, and they all went in.

"You can't just leave us in the dark like this!" Ernest exclaimed. "You've put us all in danger, for what?"

Pearlie did not respond or move an inch, and neither did any of the team members as they stood in the room, unsure of what to do next. Their eyes were drawn to the figure in the shadows, who stood motionless like a statue.

Suddenly, a gust of wind blew through the room, extinguishing the fire and plunging the room into darkness.

The team members could hear the wind whistling through the trees outside and the creak of the old wooden boards beneath their feet. The silence was almost deafening as the darkness seemed to press in on them.

"Fine, come in," Pearlie finally spoke.

They all went into the room, and before their eyes, the once-dark room began to glow with a soft blue light. The source of the light was a small, crystalline orb, floating in the air. As they watched, the orb began to expand, filling the room.

The team members felt a tingle of energy as if the air was charged with magic. Then, the orb began to spin and they saw images appearing within it. They were images of the past and of the future. They saw scenes of triumph and defeat, of love, betrayal, and loss. And as they watched, they began to understand.

As the visions faded, the team turned to the figure in the shadows. "So, it is true," Frederick said, his voice hushed. "You deceived us, Pearlie? All this time?"

Pearlie nodded slowly and pulled back her hood, revealing her guilty face. "I had my reasons," she said, but I think I'll help you this time."

"Save it, we don't need it!" Frederick interjected.

"We don't even know if we can trust you anymore," Reba said, making her way out.

Pearlie stopped the group as they were about to cross the door outside. "I promise," she started, looking pleadingly at Ernest. "I'll do it right this time, please."

Ernest gave it a serious thought before agreeing. Turning to the rest, he said, "We need her." The other two mumbled words of disapproval, but Ernest had made up his mind.

"Tell us all you know, and tell us the truth please," he said to Pearlie.

She was about to speak when a wolf emerged from the wood, fierce and angry.

"Must be the wolf that had howled at us in the woods," Reba said, tugging at the others.

But as the team stared in terror at the snarling wolf, Pearlie stepped forward. In a low, steady voice, she began to speak.

"I know this wolf," she said. "I once had a connection to its master, the dark sorcerer." The team members listened in stunned silence as she told them of her past. She had once been an apprentice to the sorcerer, but she turned against him when she realized the evil of his ways. In revenge, he had cursed her, trapping her in a half-living, half-dead state.

But now, she realized that the time had come for her to break the curse and redeem herself. "I must help Ernest find the sword," she said. "I must right the wrongs of my past."

The wolf let out a low, menacing growl, and the team tensed, ready to defend themselves. But suddenly, Pearlie held up her hand and spoke a single word, and the wolf vanished in a cloud of smoke. The team was left in shocked silence, their hearts still racing.

Then, Pearlie turned to them and said, "Now you know the truth. I ask that you help me in my pursuit for redemption as I also right my wrongs and help you find the sword."

"Tell us everything you know," Ernest said, stepping forward.

Pearlie turned to her companions and said, "The evil that is affecting Dream Haven is more powerful than you realize. It is a darkness that has been growing for many years, and it threatens to destroy all that we hold dear.

But we can overcome it. We must draw on the strength of our bond and our shared purpose. We must not give in to fear or despair. We must fight with all our hearts and minds, and we must believe in the power of hope."

The companions were silent for a moment, taking in her words.

"We will fight together," Ernest began. "And we will bring light to Dream Haven once more. But first, we must learn more about this evil that threatens us.

"What do you know of it, Pearlie?"

"I know that it is a force of darkness that has long been at work in Dream Haven," Pearlie replied. "It has been growing in power, spreading like a shadow across the land. It has brought fear and despair to the people of Dream Haven, and it seeks to control and destroy them. But I know that we can defeat it if we are united and determined."

"How about the dark sorcerer? Where does he come in this battle?" Frederick asked.

"The dark sorcerer has been terrorizing Dream Haven for too long," Pearlie continued. "I know his weaknesses, and I know how to defeat him. But I cannot do it alone. You must help me."

The team members looked at each other, their eyes wide with shock and fear. But slowly, a resolve began to grow within them.

They gathered together a few steps away from Pearlie and decided on something. "We still can't trust her, what if this is one of her old ploys?" Reba asked sardonically.

"We can never tell if we do not at least give it a shot," Ernest said convincingly.

Then, turning to Pearlie, he said, "We will help you," his voice strong and sure. "We will do whatever it takes to bring peace back to Dream Haven." The others nodded in agreement, and they knew that they were about to embark on the most dangerous journey of their lives.

With a newfound sense of purpose, the team set out from the clearing, following Pearlie's directions. The road they traveled was dark and foreboding, and they felt as if they were being watched by unseen eyes. But they pressed on, determined to see their mission through.

"Why does this road seem so different from the ones we'd traveled through all day long?" Reba asked inquisitively.

"Because this road is often hidden from the sight of men by the powers of magic," Pearlie revealed, still leading them on.

Finally, they reached the edge of a dark forest, and they paused, unsure of what lay ahead. Then, they saw a dim light flickering in the distance, and they knew they had found their destination.

"That must be the sorcerer's lair," Pearlie said.

"Are you asking or telling? Because if you are asking, how are we supposed to know?" Frederick asked.

"It is here that our journey will reach its climax," Pearlie answered, not so much as glancing at Frederick.

As they approached the light, they saw that it was coming from a small hut, half-hidden among the trees. They could hear strange sounds coming from within, and a chill ran down their spines. But they knew they could not turn back now. They steeled themselves and approached the door.

"What do we do?" Ernest whispered.

"We must go in," Pearlie said, her voice steady. "We must confront the sorcerer and end his reign of terror." And with that, she pushed open the door and led the way inside.

As they stepped into the hut, they were struck by a wave of cold air.

The air was thick with the smell of incense and decay, and the floor was covered in bones and strange markings. But what truly shocked them was the figure they saw sitting in the center of the room.

It was the dark sorcerer, his face hidden by a hooded cloak, his eyes glowing with a dark light. "So, you have come," he said, his voice deep and resonant. "You are brave but foolish. You cannot hope to defeat me."

The team members stood their ground, their resolve tested by the sorcerer's magic, but they knew they would be successful because they had Pearlie with them.

The sorcerer rose from his chair and a strange light began to emanate from his hands. "You are but pawns in a much larger game," he said. "A game that has been played for millennia. A game that you cannot hope to win."

The team members began to feel a sense of despair, but they fought to keep their courage. "We will not give up," the team leader said, his voice shaking. "We will fight until the end."

In the midst of the confrontation, the group of four suddenly felt their eyelids grow heavy, and they found themselves unable to keep their eyes open.

Slowly, they drifted into a deep sleep as the dark sorcerer began to weave a dream around them. "Steady, everyone! Try not to succumb to sleep," Pearlie warned.

"What's happening?" Reba asked.

"I can barely keep my eyes open!" Frederick said with sleep in his eyes. A yawn escaped his mouth and he dozed off quickly.

"Keep your eyes open, guys, please," Pearlie pleaded. "This evil man is playing with you, stay awake," she said, but was slowly drifting off herself.

The dark sorcerer began to laugh as he toyed with their subconscious minds.

As they drifted off, snoring in the process, they found themselves standing in the midst of a vast, desolate wasteland. The sky was dark and cloudy, and the ground was scorched and barren.

"I've seen this before," Pearlie said to the others.

A wind howled through the air, carrying with it a faint, whispering voice. "You are mine now," the voice said, and the four of them began to feel a sense of dread. But then, they heard Pearlie's voice, and it seemed to drown the first.

"You can resist," she said, and the team members felt a surge of strength and courage. They looked at each other, and they knew that they could not give in to the darkness.

Pearlie's voice was like the voice of hope as it grew louder until it was like a song that filled the sky. It began to weave a new dream around them—a dream of a beautiful, lush forest.

Birds sang in the branches, and a river flowed nearby, its waters sparkling like diamonds. The team members felt their spirits lifted, and they knew that they could overcome anything.

"I am with you all, just stick with me," Pearlie continued, and with that, she disappeared from their sights in the dream.

And immediately, her consciousness returned with her from the world of illusion back to where the dark sorcerer stood.

Glancing over the sleeping bodies of the three travelers, she looked over their faces and said some spell over them.

"Wake up!" she commanded, and the team roused immediately.

With that, the sorcerer let out a roar of rage, and the battle began, but Pearlie stepped in to confront the sorcerer.

Ernest, Frederick, and Reba shifted from the ground and found a safe spot to watch the two fight each other.

As Pearlie and the dark sorcerer faced each other, the air around them crackled with energy. Dark lightning flashed, illuminating their faces.

As the battle raged on, the team members realized that they could not defeat the sorcerer alone. They needed to work together to pool their strength and their will.

"Give up, Pearlie," the dark sorcerer said, his voice low and menacing. "You cannot win against me, and you know that. What student fights his teacher?"

"You're wrong," Pearlie replied, her voice steady. "I have something you don't." "What could that be?" the dark sorcerer sneered.

"A clear conscience—something you can never boast about," Pearlie said, and with that, a white light began to glow around her.

All this while, the others had been watching with keen interest and optimism. If Pearlie loses the fight, they're in trouble seeing as they're already in the lion's den, adding that they had already witnessed how much the dark sorcerer could do when he infiltrated their dreams.

The white light grew brighter and brighter until it was blinding. The dark sorcerer covered his eyes, but the light burned through his hands, scorching his skin. He screamed in pain and fell to his knees. "Love conquers all," Pearlie said as the light began to dim.

She approached the dark sorcerer, who cowered before her. "I will not harm you," she said. "But you must repent of your actions."

The dark sorcerer hung his head, and tears began to fall from his eyes. "I will do whatever it takes to make amends," he said, his voice breaking.

Pearlie placed her hand on the dark sorcerer's shoulder, and a warm, comforting light began to spread from her palm. The dark sorcerer felt the pain and anger leave his body, and in its place was a deep sense of peace.

He looked up at Pearlie, his eyes brimming with gratitude. "Thank you," he said, his voice thick with emotion. "You have shown me the true power of love, and I will never forget it."

"Better not," Frederick said behind Pearlie, and the group stepped out of the dark sorcerer's hut.

After going a good long way, Pearlie stopped in her tracks and said to the others, "Now that I've helped you in your quest, do I at least get a small amount of your trust and friendship?"

"You mean we've helped you defeat the dark sorcerer and free yourself? You should be grateful to us," Frederick said, and Reba gave him a light hit on the stomach.

"Shuuush, shut it!" she warned. "Oouch!" he cried, his mouth wide open.

"We'll keep in mind what you've done for us," Ernest said, and they all waved her goodbye and started leaving while Ernest stayed back.

"Let me know if you ever need my help finding the sword in the future. I'll be more than eager to assist," she said to them. Then, to Ernest, she turned and said, "Thank you for believing in me."

"Sure!" Ernest said, giving her a light pat on the shoulder. "Come on, Ernest. We need to go!" Frederick shouted to him.

As he joined them on the way, the trio knew that one thing was certain, they were headed right for the sword, and nothing was going to stand in their way.

CHAPTER 10

THROUGH WHISPERING WOODS

The warm air blew a still breeze past the trio as they weaved their way through a forest, but there was a strange, electric charge in the atmosphere. A storm was brewing, and the air felt heavy with it. The sky was a deep, brooding gray, and the clouds were dark and threatening, yet there was no drop of rain.

The forest was unlike any they had ever seen. The trees were tall and ancient, their leaves a deep, rich green. The ground was covered in a carpet of soft moss, and the air was filled with the scent of wildflowers. But as they walked, they began to feel a strange sense of unease. The air was too still— too quiet. The trees seemed to be watching them, and the shadows were just a little too dark.

Ernest, Frederick, and Reba found themselves in the midst of an ancient forest, its trees towering overhead and its branches entwined like a maze.

The air was still and quiet, and a strange feeling of calm settled over them. But something felt off. The forest was too quiet, too still. The trees seemed to be watching them, their branches reaching out like grasping fingers. The three companions felt a sense of unease, and they knew that they had to be on their guard. Suddenly, they heard a low growl and froze in their tracks.

"What was that?" whispered Reba, wide-eyed.

"I don't know," said Ernest, his voice shaking. "But we need to be careful. We're not alone here." "We should keep moving," Frederick said, his hand reaching for his sword. "But stay alert."

"Agreed," said Ernest. "Stay close to each other. And whatever happens, don't let go of my hand," he added, looking at the fear-stricken Reba.

She nodded, and they moved slowly and cautiously through the forest, their hearts pounding in their chests. Every step felt like a mile, and the shadows seemed to loom larger and darker.

Then, without warning, the shadows around them began to move. They heard a rustling in the leaves and a low growl. Suddenly, a pack of wolves burst out of the trees, their eyes glowing red and their teeth bared. The companions were frozen in terror, and for a moment, they could not move. But then, with a shout, Ernest drew his sword and charged at the wolves. The others followed, fighting for their lives.

Amidst the chaos, they could hear a howl rising above the noise—a howl that sent shivers down their spines. Then they heard a low, seductive voice whispering in their ears. "You cannot win," it said. "Why not give up and rest? You are tired, and this is too much for you. Let go of your worries and your fears. Let go and sleep."

"No!" cried Ernest, fighting against the voice. "We must keep going. We must fight."

"You cannot fight forever," the voice purred. "Why not rest? It would feel so good to stop, to give up. The forest is so welcoming, so peaceful," the voice coaxed on.

"The forest is not peaceful! It is trying to deceive us, to lure us into a false sense of security. We must resist!" Ernest shouted even louder, his eyes burning with determination as he turned to stare at the rest.

"You must listen to me," he said. "I know what we must do. We must stay together and keep moving forward. We must not stop, no matter what. We must stay focused on our goal, and we must resist the temptation of the forest."

The others nodded, their resolve strengthened by his words. And then, from somewhere deep within the trees, they heard a sound. It was faint at first, but it grew steadily louder. It was a voice, one that filled them with hope. A voice that sang of courage and strength.

"I am here," it said. "To guide you on your way. I will not leave you, and I will not fail you. Trust in me and we will overcome all obstacles. Trust, and we will win."

After the voice, a figure appeared in the midst of the trees—a woman dressed in flowing robes of emerald green. She stood before them, her face radiant, her eyes filled with compassion.

"Greetings, brave ones," she said. "I am the Guardian of the Forest, and I have come to offer you my guidance," she started. "Put your swords away, you can trust me."

Ernest put his sword back into the sheath, and the others followed suit.

"But before I can do so, you must face your true selves, your deepest fears and doubts," the Guardian of the Forest continued. "You must confront your inner darkness, and only then will you be able to proceed."

The three exchanged nervous glances, unsure of what to do. "We need more clarity here," Frederick said.

"Do not fear," the guardian said, sensing their unease. "I am here to help you, not to harm you. I will guide you on a journey of self-discovery, a journey that will take you to your very core. There, you will find your true selves, and only then will you be able to face what lies ahead."

"What lies ahead?" Ernest asked, his voice quivering.

"To get to your destination and retrieve the sword, which is beyond the forest, beyond even the wildest reaches of your imagination," the guardian replied. "You must first journey within," she finished.

The trio looked at each other once more, their hearts racing. "We are ready," Ernest said, his voice trembling but firm. The others nodded in agreement.

"Then close your eyes," the guardian said. "Imagine yourself at the edge of a great chasm. This chasm represents your inner self, the deepest, most hidden parts of your soul. You must jump into the chasm, and you must not be afraid. For I will be with you, and you will not fall."

They closed their eyes, took a deep breath, and then leaped. They fell through darkness, through swirling images and memories. They saw themselves as children, they saw their joys and sorrows. They saw their deepest fears, their most secret dreams. And then, they landed in a city that seemed quite surreal, although they knew it was only an illusion.

As they entered the city, they found themselves in a great hall, its walls lined with mirrors. They saw their reflections staring back at them, but their reflections were not as they expected. Instead of seeing their own faces, they saw their deepest fears, their darkest secrets. One by one, they saw the reflections change.

And the guardian's voice whispered in their ears, guiding them, reassuring them. "Do not be afraid," the voice said. "For in your vulnerability lies your strength. In your weakness, you will find your true power."

Ernest saw himself as a child, standing alone in a dark room. He saw himself growing up, always feeling alone and isolated. But then, he saw himself surrounded by friends and family, all of them smiling and laughing. He saw himself as a strong and confident leader, guiding others with wisdom and compassion. And when the reflection faded, he knew that he had faced his true self and come out stronger.

The next reflection to change was Reba's, who saw herself as a child, playing in the mud and laughing with reckless abandon. But then, the reflection shifted, and she saw herself as a teenager, angry and sullen. She saw herself pushing away those who cared about her, pushing them away with her anger and bitterness, which was what she'd done as a teenager.

But then, the reflection changed again, and she saw herself as an adult, her face lined with wisdom and maturity. She saw herself surrounded by friends and family, all of them loving and supporting her.

And when the reflection faded, she knew that she had faced her true self, and she had come out stronger.

Frederick also saw himself as a child, always seeking the approval of others. But then, the reflection shifted and he saw himself as a young man, always putting the needs of others before his own.

He saw himself as a fierce and loyal protector, always standing up for those who could not stand up for themselves.

But then, the reflection changed again, and he saw himself as an old man, tired and weary. He saw himself as a man who had given everything for the sake of others, and he felt a deep sense of satisfaction.

And when the reflection faded, he knew that he had faced his true self, and he had come out stronger. He felt a new sense of purpose and resolve, and he knew that he would never waver from his duty.

The group stood together, united and determined. They had faced their true selves, and they emerged stronger and more united. They were ready for whatever the world had in store for them.

And then, the darkness began to fade and they found themselves standing on solid ground once more. "Were we successful?" Reba asked as they all awoke from their test.

The Guardian of the Forest didn't respond immediately, she only stood before them, her face glowing with love and understanding.

"Welcome back," she then said. "You have faced your innermost fears, and you have emerged stronger and more whole. Are you ready to proceed?"

"Yes," they all chorused in unison, their voices strong and steady. "We are ready."

"Then come with me," the guardian said. "We have much to do, and time is short." And with that, they set off into the forest, the guardian leading the way.

As they walked, the group began to notice a curious thing. The further they went, the darker the sky became until it was nearly nighttime. The wind began to howl, and the leaves rustled with an eerie, whispering sound.

The rain fell harder and the air was filled with the scent of ozone. But the group followed the guardian without hesitation, trusting in her guidance. And then, they reached the heart of the forest, a clearing that seemed somehow out of time.

"This is the place," the guardian said. "This is where your true test will begin." "Again? I thought we'd passed the only test," Reba complained.

"No, that wasn't a test. It was helping you find yourself, now is the real test."

The group stood at the edge of the clearing, their hearts pounding. The air was thick with magic, and the trees seemed to loom over them like living, breathing creatures.

The rain stopped, and the clearing was bathed in a strange, silvery light. In the center of the clearing stood a great stone altar, its surface covered in runes and symbols. The guardian gestured to the altar, and the companions approached it.

"Place your hands upon the altar," she said. "And be prepared for what comes next."

The group did as she said, their hands trembling as they touched the cold, smooth stone.

As they placed their hands on the altar, a jolt of energy shot through them like lightning running through their veins. The air around them began to swirl, and the clearing seemed to spin and shift. When the spinning stopped, they found themselves in a strange, otherworldly place.

The sky was purple and streaked with stars, and the ground was made of sparkling, iridescent sand. In the distance, they could see a tall, majestic tower, its spires reaching up into the sky.

"Welcome to the Tower of Truth," the guardian said. "This is where your journey truly begins."

As they approached the tower, they could see that its walls were made of shimmering, translucent crystal. And inside the crystal, they could see strange, shadowy shapes moving. They felt a deep sense of trepidation as they entered the tower, the crystal door closing behind them with a soft click. As they stood in the center, they saw a staircase spiraling upwards, leading to a platform far above.

"You must climb the stairs," the guardian said. "Only at the top will you find what you seek."

As they began to climb, their legs started shaking with each step. The air around them seemed to grow thinner as they got higher, and they found themselves gasping for breath. But they did not stop, driven by a fierce determination. Finally, they reached the top of the staircase and found themselves in a round, empty room.

In the center of the room stood a pedestal, upon which rested a glowing crystal orb. "You must gaze into the orb," the guardian said. "It will show you the truth of your quest."

Nervously, the group approached the pedestal. They gazed into the orb and saw a vision of a terrible battle. They saw their friends and allies, their faces twisted with fear and pain.

They saw the forces of darkness, a horde of terrible creatures and terrifying sorcerers. And at the center of it all, they saw the sorcerer, his face a mask of rage and hatred. They watched in horror as the battle erupted until, finally, it came to a terrible conclusion. When the vision ended, they turned to the guardian, their eyes wide with fear.

"What does it mean?" Ernest asked.

"It means that the time of testing is upon you," the guardian replied. "You must prepare for battle. You must hone your skills and train your minds and bodies. For only then will you have any hope of victory."

The group looked at each other, their faces grim and determined. "We are ready," Frederick said with renewed confidence. "We will not falter. We will not fail."

"Good," the guardian said. "For the fate of Dream Haven rests in your hands."

With that, the guardian disappeared and the room around them began to shift and change. They found themselves back in the clearing, the crystal door standing open before them.

But the clearing was different, transformed by the magic that had passed through it. The air was thick with power, and the trees seemed to stand taller and straighter. On the ground, a new flower had sprung up, its petals glowing with a pure, white light.

"Take the flower," a voice whispered. "It will give you strength and courage."

They reached down and picked the flower, its petals soft and delicate in their hands. As they held it, they felt a surge of divine power flowing through them, filling them with a sense of purpose and resolve. They knew what they must do. They turned to each other and nodded, a silent agreement passing between them. And then, they began to walk back through the forest, the flower held close to their hearts.

As they walked, they felt the weight of their responsibility, but they also felt a deep sense of hope. They knew that they could do this, that they could overcome all obstacles.

As they reached the edge of the forest, they saw a vast plain stretching out before them. And in the distance, they saw a great city, its towers and walls gleaming in the sun. When they drew closer, they saw that the city was teeming with life, its streets bustling with activity.

At its center, they saw a great castle, its walls rising high into the sky. They approached the castle gates and saw a figure standing there, waiting for them. The figure was tall and regal, dressed in flowing robes of blue and silver—it was a woman, her features ageless and beautiful. She held out her hand and they saw that she was holding a golden key.

"Welcome, heroes," she said, her voice filled with warmth. "I have been waiting for you. You have a great task ahead of you, but I have faith that you will succeed. Enter the city and begin your journey."

They took the key from her hand and felt its power flowing through them. They turned to the city gates and saw that they were open, beckoning them to enter.

They walked through the gates and were met with a sound like nothing they had ever heard before. It was a strange, unearthly melody, and it seemed to be coming from all around them, drawing them towards its source.

"The sound seems to be coming from this way," Reba said, listening closely.

So, they followed the sound and found themselves in a large square, surrounded by towering buildings. In the center of the square, they saw a massive tree, its branches reaching towards the sky. And sitting in the branches of the tree was a small, delicate creature, singing a strange melody.

As they approached the tree, the small creature stopped singing and looked down at them. It was a tiny fairy, its wings fluttering gently in the breeze.

"Greetings, heroes," the fairy said. "I am the Guardian of the Tree of Songs, and I am honored to meet you. You are seeking the sword, I see. But before you can claim the sword, you must learn its story. Will you listen?"

"Yes, we will," said Ernest, speaking for the group. "We are eager to learn all we can."

And so, the fairy began to tell them the story of the sword. "Long ago, in a time of darkness, there lived a great hero. This hero was fearless and strong, and he was loved by all. But one day, the hero was faced with a terrible foe—a creature of darkness and evil. The hero fought bravely, but he could not defeat the creature.

He was on the brink of defeat when a small, silver sword appeared in front of him. The sword glowed with a holy light, and it gave the hero the strength to defeat the creature.

And so, the hero became known as the Swordbearer, and he used the sword to bring peace and light to the land. But one day, the sword was stolen, and the Swordbearer was unable to find it. The sword had fallen into the hands of the enemy, and the land was once again plunged into darkness.

The Swordbearer was devastated and vowed to find the sword and restore the land to its former glory. And so, he set out on a quest, following every clue and searching every corner of the land. But no matter where he looked, the sword could not be found. The years passed and the Swordbearer grew old, but still, he never found it."

Ernest, Reba, and Frederick listened to the Guardian of the Tree of Songs' story with rapt attention, not daring to miss out on any detail.

"That means the sword has not been found yet?" Reba asked.

"It will be... by you," the guardian said. "I know you seek the sword, but it is not an easy path. You must travel to the land of shadows, where darkness reigns. You must face your fears, and only then will you find what you seek."

"Do we always have to face our fears? We've faced like a thousand fears already on this journey," Frederick retorted with mixed feelings.

"Does it get any less scary?" Reba interjected.

"That is the only way to possess the sword and free the people from the reign of terror forever. Only then will you truly find your purpose and live satisfactorily," the guardian said and was gone in an instant.

The team members braced themselves for the difficult journey ahead, knowing that only by facing their fears could they find the sword.

"You guys ready?" Ernest asked and they nodded. "We can do this together if we have no doubt but faith in our journey," he assured them.

"This is only getting more and more interesting," Reba said with a laugh. "I bet I'll love this next phase or whatever we'll face."

"Luckily, we won't have to face any of our fears anymore," Frederick said with a wry laugh and the crew laughed along.

With that, they set off, traveling through forests and mountains, encountering all manner of strange creatures and obstacles.

Finally, they would reach the land of shadows—a dark and foreboding place. There, they would face their greatest challenges yet. But through it all, they would remember the words of the tree of songs, and they would find the strength to persevere. And at last, they would find the sword, its light burning bright in the darkness.

As the team continued on their way, Ernest knew in his heart that a lot had changed. He had changed… he was more than just the orphan boy who began this journey.

Although he kept it in his heart, he had always felt like he was defined by his past, that he was unwanted and uncared for, but facing his true self made him realize that he could be more than his circumstances.

He could be a hero, a seeker of truth, and he could be more if he was willing to accept that challenge, and he knew he was ready.

He would rather win this battle than stay the same, and winning is what he was most determined to do as he walked the path with his crew and friends.

"All roads lead to the sword," Frederick said suddenly, and Reba laughed.

"I can't wait to see what it looks like," she started. "Do you ever have a mental picture of what the sword looks like?" she asked no one in particular.

"A lot," Ernest replied. "But I'm going to see if I was correct all along," he said with his eyes on the road ahead.

CHAPTER 11

EDGE OF REALITY

The dark purple sun hung low in the sky, casting an unnatural hue about the land of shadows. It kept the land in a state of perpetual darkness. They had long learned that magic would have caused this strange phenomenon. The group entered the lands when it was a bright morning, yet it seemed as though it was evening. For the sun cast a perpetual hue on the land. The trees were larger and had dark purple light running through them from root to leaves. They would be sure that all the animals that lay within the land were infected with the strange light.

The group made their way, slowly at first, to the tower that would serve as the resting place for the sword. They forged through the dense sleep-packed vegetation of the forest, taking little breaks. Every now and then, a small shadow creature would attack them, slowing them down all the more. By the third day, they had long since run out of physical energy, the food rations were depleted, and they were running out of water. There was something about the land of the shadows, but sleep hung heavy in their eyes.

They knew that by surrendering to it, they would give way to the sorcerer. So, they stole their heart and unfortunately, their heads. At some point on the fourth day, they would get attacked by creatures of the shadow—creatures that were corrupted with the shadow blight. They looked like normal creatures, except that they were larger like the trees. Even a smaller rabbit would have sharp teeth and claws, it would be larger than an average dog. Aside from fighting for their lives, the group forced themselves to stay awake.

"Open your eyes! You'll let him in!" Ernest yelled, snapping them out of their slumber. The damage was done, however, as the forest around them began to warp and change before their very eyes. The scene kept unfolding into different mirages and different versions. And when the strange movement stopped, they did not recognize the place before them.

Ernest sent a knowing smile to his companions—he too was fighting the same battle. "Oh no," voiced Reba, taking in the scene. "I'm sorry. This is my fault."

Ernest shook his head, causing his hair to move in the strange wind. "It's not you, it's this place. We're in his backyard." He put down his bags and began to climb the nearest tall tree, hoping to find their way by seeing the sun.

Frederick looked at him with a worried face. "For some reason, they're active during the day." He handed Ernest a dagger. "You know what to do." Earning a nod from the lad. He disappeared into the canopy of trees above. They both watched Ernest as he made his way up the cursed tree. Trusting him, they stood guard on the ground below. A while later, Ernest landed on the ground with a soft thud.

"The tower is that way," he said, pointing left. They made haste, hoping to cover as much ground as possible to defeat as many of the shadow creatures as they could.

Wave after wave, shadow creatures came after them. It seemed, however, that the group was already used to fighting them.

Sensing that the sorcerer sent them a new type of enemy to deal with.

This time, it was the guardian. A lookalike of the guardian, at least, but they knew better... they knew that she wouldn't be there. The creature before them was portrayed by her in gold and the strange purple and was veined with the blight. "What you are looking for is not here," it said. "You are wasting your time, come with me. I will show you something." The illusion had a very similar voice to that of the real guardian.

"Don't listen to it, it's an illusion," Ernest said. The slightly mocking smile of the figure changed to a grotesque mask of horror.

"You will die here!" it said before vanishing from their sight.

In the coming days, the trio faced terrifying illusions that brought to question their sanity and trust for one another.

The one before them now was the hulking form of a Dreamcatcher, but several times larger than the average one. This one tested their limits, forcing them to push their bodies beyond exhaustion.

The mirage of the 20-foot soldier charged at them, laying waste to trees and smaller shadow creatures. Reba hung back, playing with the lack of light, she thrived in secrecy. She pulled out her throwing knives and her crossbow, fighting the beast in her way.

Ernest darted between its legs, catching its attention, his slim figure wielding his twin daggers to perfection. He cut the creature at its kneecap, sending it to the ground.

The illusion was slow and bulky. Its hands were flying about, trying to swat Ernest off like he was a fly. Frederick brandished his broadsword, going in for the kill. He swung at the head of the colossal soldier, slicing it. It faded into nothing... only to respawn.

"I guess we have to kill it again," Frederick remarked, to which Ernest chuckled in reply. They prepared to face it a second time.

This time, Reba focused her attacks on the feet of the

Dreamcatcher, causing the illusion to stomp about the forest, hitting trees. In an effortless stroke, Frederick, once again, sliced off the head of the illusion.

It respawned again, which warranted a groan from Reba. "How many more times do we have to kill this thing?" she asked.

Frederick stood resolute, the dark magic attempting to twist his perceptions snaked around his body. He shrugged it off but it kept at him, leaving him out of the fight. Dark magic attempted to twist his perceptions, but his unwavering sense of duty shielded him from the illusions.

With a mighty roar, he charged towards the towering enemy, his sword gleaming with the light of a thousand stars. Each clash of blades echoed through the illusions, resonating with the determination to protect his comrades.

The battle reached a crescendo—a symphony of steel, shadows, and magic. Ernest danced between reality and illusion, Reba exploited the chaos to her advantage, and Frederick stood as an unyielding bastion against the dark forces. Together, they orchestrated a harmonious assault, further increasing their battle strength and exploiting the intricacies of the magical battlefield.

As the moon dipped below the horizon, the colossal soldier stumbled, defeated by the collective prowess of the trio. The illusions dissipated, revealing a battlefield transformed by their collaboration. The trio stood victorious—a testament to the power of skill, cunning, and noble valor in the face of dark magic.

The illusion of the battle cleared, leaving them before the tower's gates. The group panted, sharing a look between themselves. They knew they couldn't stop to rest. The sorcerer knew they were close to the sword, for they remained just beyond his grasp. Together, they walked into the tower.

Total darkness covered Ernest as he doubted whether he was awake. "Frederick! Reba!" he yelled at the top of his lungs.

"Ernest?!" Reba's scared voice answered, followed by Frederick's. Ernest heaved a sigh of relief. His worries started.

Knowing that they were safe, he felt the darkness around him, reaching for nothing but everything. A cool, rough surface reached his fingertips.

He let his hands lead him further into the darkness, as did Frederick and Reba. A heavy sleep almost claimed them further into the dark maze, whispers from the sorcerer flooded their ears, edging them on to the sweetness of slumber, but they remained true to their quest, reaching to the inner strength they all had and forging ahead.

Knowing that his whispers could not entice them, the sorcerer sent his nightmares after them, thickening the darkness around them some more. He was sure they'd never find the sword. But he was wrong, the trio progressed closer to the sword's resting place, eliminating all enemies he sent their way.

Ernest heard panting beside his own. "Ernie?" whispered the feminine voice. Ernest released his breath. "Where is Frederick?" she asked, her eyes picking out his faint shape in the dark.

"The darkness is leaving," breathed the deep voice of Frederick. They all tensed, ready for battle. Knowing the sorcerer, he would never let them take his most prized possession without a fight. And they did get into a fight. The darkness was pulled away harshly, coming together to form a visage of the sorcerer. His menacingly hooded figure towered before them.

"Never has anyone made it this far. I laud you, heroes." The voice that came from the hooded form was deep, angry, and menacing, spoken with a thousand whispers behind it, luring them to sleep. "But

this is as far as you go. You will die here!" Dark tendrils of magic wove out from the figure. They tried to cut the weaves, but it snaked around them and entered their mouths.

They opened their eyes to see a starless sky reflecting off an eerily calm black ocean.

The illumination came from a large moon hanging in the sky above. The sorcerer's form rose from the inky surface, being darkness himself. "Alas, you are finally home." He raised his hood from his head, revealing a pale bald head beneath it. Black soulless eyes stared at them, hypnotizing them. Inky hands opened his pale, thin lips, widening them beyond anything humanly possible, reaching for them.

Ernest reached out to hold Reba's cold hands and Frederick's. Together, they would beat him. Within their dreams, the sorcerer was powerful, but so were they, together. The reaching hands never touched them. A shield of blue light was about them.

"How did you learn that power?! Wh—the fairies mu—"

As the trio stood before the deranged man, they couldn't help but wonder what he was muttering to himself. His wild eyes darted around frantically, his lips moving silently as if he were trying to summon some unseen force. It was clear that this man had spent far too many years consumed by his thirst for power, and now it seemed that obsession had driven him completely mad.

Suddenly, without warning, the crazed sorcerer lunged at them in a frenzy of movement. The trio braced themselves for impact, but it was Frederick who reacted first. With a fierce battle cry, he charged at the madman, brandishing his broadsword with all his might.

The two clashed in a blur of steel and magic. Sparks flew as Frederick's blade met the sorcerer's dark form, and for a moment, it seemed as though they were evenly matched.

But then something changed... something shifted within Frederick. Suddenly, he felt a surge of holy power coursing through him, filling him with an otherworldly strength.

With renewed vigor, Frederick slashed through the sorcerer's defenses like a hot knife through butter. The man screamed in agony as he fell to the ground defeated, his once fearsome powers now nothing more than ashes in the wind.

They woke up from their slumber, knowing that he was

merely weakened. They would fight him again. And they would win.

Getting up, they beheld the sight of colossal stone doors. The carvings on the stone are reminiscent of the same tower in their trials. It bore them no ill will. It was waiting for a worthy hero to free it from the clutches of darkness. For millennia, it lay in darkness for that long. But hope always stirred within as the heroes attempted to open the heavy weight of its prison.

They pushed the door with their might. The only reward for their hard work being the slight croaking of the stone. Pushing some more, the stone doors moved. "One more!" Frederick said. The vein on his temple bulged in recognition. They pushed once more and the doors opened just enough for each of them to squeeze through.

Ernest cautiously made his way into the cavern, his sword casting an illuminating light that pierced through the darkness. He moved with such delicacy that it seemed as though he was afraid to disturb the stillness of the space. As his eyes scanned the surroundings, he took in the enormity of the hall— its 20-foot-high ceiling adorned with verdant green moss that glistened in the light. The walls were lined with thick vines that had crept down over time and caused cracks to appear in some areas.

The only sounds that could be heard were Ernest's breathing and the gentle hum emanating from the sword, which rested on a raised stone platform at the center of the room. As he approached, he noticed how gracefully water lapped against the rock beneath him. The atmosphere was eerie yet mesmerizing all at once.

Reba's voice echoed through the ancient hall, dripping with sarcasm as she declared, "Any time today." Frederick smiled faintly and shook his head at her impatience. She paced back and forth along the stony floor, urging them to hurry up. "It's not like you need a ceremony to pick up the sword," she added.

Ernest stepped forward, his confidence bolstered by his previous encounter with the guardian. Frederick and Reba followed silently behind him, encouraging him to move closer to the pool of water ahead.

As Ernest reached the edge of the clear pool, he took off his old boots and rolled up his trousers— borrowed from Frederick— revealing his slim calves. The warm water lapped gently against his skin as he waded through it towards the small island where the sword lay.

The sight that greeted Ernest was breathtaking. The holy power within the sword pulsed like a beating heart, filling him with a sense of calm and tranquility. He continued waddling closer until he reached the island's center.

He climbed up the stone platform. The hum of the sword was much louder, almost deafening now. The hum resonated with the power within him. It tugged at him, edging him to pick it up, to be worthy of its power, to be the true hero.

He picked up the sword. Its weight was lighter than the average sword but almost the length of a longsword. The steel glowed with an ethereal blue light of magic.

The humming sound that had filled the air suddenly stopped, and the soft glow emanating from the sword slowly faded away. Ernest frowned to himself as he realized that the sword now looked like any other ordinary one. He could sense Frederick's presence beside him and they shared a glance, both feeling anxious about what this meant for their mission.

Reba's voice betrayed her anxiety as she asked, "What is it?" The heaviness in the air was palpable and it was clear that she needed no answer. Ernest carefully handed over the sword before putting on his shoes. To Reba, it appeared to be a regular sword— albeit a rather fanciful one with an embellished silver hilt studded with jewels.

The soft light that had once emitted from it was now gone. It was then that Ernest spoke, "He tricked us. The map... everything was just a ruse." They all knew that the only real things they encountered were the guardian and fairies.

Reba's fear became apparent as she croaked out, "So, what do we do now?"

Frederick glanced at them both before sizing up Ernest, who leaned against the wet stone wall. After a moment of contemplation, he replied, "Well, we can't fight the sorcerer now. Not without the real sword. The form he showed us was simply an illusion… it did not give us an accurate estimation of his true strength."

Out of the three of them, Ernest appeared to be physically shaken by this revelation as he had genuinely hoped that they would find the sword here and finally put an end to their nemesis once and for all. Shivers ran through his thin frame, and sensing this, Frederick pulled him into an embrace— one that Reba did not hesitate to join in as well, for they all needed warmth and comfort in this dark time.

The trio stayed like that for what seemed like an eternity in the cold stone caverns where they were left with nothing but their thoughts and fears about what lay ahead in their quest to defeat the sorcerer. As for that moment, the stone cavern only made them sour.

Exiting the tower was no easy feat for the trio as they found themselves in a maze filled with shadowy creatures and beasts that seemed to have come straight out of their nightmares. Ernest, who was feeling a different kind of exhaustion, was struggling to keep up with his companions.

The maze offered him no comfort and the mere thought of training with his sword left him feeling weak and drained. He had no idea where he would find the strength to continue, but he knew that he couldn't give up.

Remembering his duty, he steeled himself and hardened his face, determined not to let weakness get the best of him. His mission was too important for him to fail, and the darkness of the maze would not be his final resting place.

When they finally emerged from the tower, it was clear that

they had been through a grueling battle. Frederick was nursing an injury to his right arm, likely sustained during their fight. Ernest was limping badly, and Reba was bleeding from multiple cuts all over her body. They were all in need of rest and healing, but their sense of urgency compelled them to push forward.

Frederick bound his dislocated shoulder with a grimace while Ernest tended to his swollen left leg. Reba seemed to have fared better than her companions, sustaining only scratches and bruises. As she picked up the fake sword from where he had laid it down, she commented on its quality and how it could fetch a good price if sold in Dream Haven. The men avoided her gaze as she rambled on about its worth as a collector's item for some wealthy elite.

Ernest eventually took back his sword from Reba's hand and strapped it securely onto his back using a makeshift handle. It was time for them to move on, despite their injuries and weariness. They knew that there were more challenges ahead of them before they could complete their mission successfully. But with determination in their hearts, they set off into the distance once again.

The heroes found themselves disappointingly distant from their heroic aspirations. The coveted sword, a symbol of their potential greatness, lay ensnared within the clutches of the malevolent sorcerer. A melancholic scene unfolded, the weapon yearning for liberation, its metallic essence echoing a silent plea for salvation. If only the heroes comprehended the latent power residing within them—a dormant strength capable of lifting the sword from its somber captivity.

The blade, resonating with an aura of anticipation, trembled with hope, longing for the moment it could taste the sweet air of freedom. A silent yearning emanated from the sword as if it sought to convey the vivid images of its constrained existence, painting a vivid picture of entrapment and longing. It yearned for the touch of a new wielder, particularly one who could resonate with the echoes of its past master.

The youthful hero, seemingly unaware of his latent potential, stood as a beacon of hope for the enchanted weapon. There was an uncanny resemblance between the boy and the sword's former master—a connection that transcended the passage of time. The sword envisioned a future where the young one would master its ancient ways, a journey that involved not only the art of swordsmanship but also the profound understanding of divine powers.

The burden of this imminent task weighed heavily on the blade's essence. It recognized the formidable challenge awaiting the young hero, a challenge that required not only mastering the intricate techniques of swordplay but also unlocking the mysteries of the power of dreams. The sword whispered ancient wisdom to the boy—a subtle guidance urging him to embark on the arduous journey of self-discovery.

The steel was more than just a mere object—it was a relic of the past, holding within it memories of a time long gone by. It remembered the days when hope still shone bright and the future seemed limitless... before darkness snatched it from the embrace of light, plunging everything into chaos and despair. In those darkest moments, however, there were heroes like the boy who stood before their quests with determination, seekers of truth who sought freedom and justice for all. The boy, now spindly and light for his age, had a fierce determination burning deep within him.

As he grew older, that determination only grew stronger until he became a true force to be reckoned with—a mighty warrior who slayed the most terrible nightmares that plagued their people. His bravery and strength ushered in an era of hope and peace for a brief moment in time. The common folk could dream as they wished and bask in sweet light.

But nothing good lasts forever...

The day turned cold under the dream field. Nights turned to nightmares—a time when the hero's sword was taken from him. His name echoed through history as he fought with every last breath to retrieve

it from the source's forces but failed until his death. For centuries upon centuries thereafter, this deal waited within the depths of darkness for another worthy soul to come forth and take up its challenge.

And eventually, someone did come forth. After lying dormant for so long, it was finally discovered once more—within the depth of dreams. It was waiting patiently for someone brave enough to wield it again, someone strong enough to face whatever horrors might come their way. And one day soon, they would find it, ready to embark on their journey towards greatness and honor.

CHAPTER 12

A SINISTER SMILE

Beads of perspiration adorned the man's plump, rosy cheeks, drenched in the anxiety that clung to him. Labored breaths escaped his stout frame as his fingers tightly clutched the weighty silk robes. Fear consumed him—an unusual state for the typically composed sorcerer.

Observing his enraged master pacing across the marble expanse of the dream realm, the man, afraid to speak, marveled at the oddity. The corpulent noble had crafted this dreamscape as a perpetual display of opulence, an ostentatious showcase for his lavish fantasies. Within this surreal world, dreams were spun, embellished with jewels and art, destined to materialize at the grand soirées of high society.

Tonight, however, the presence of his Dark Lord stripped his walls down to a pale imitation of its former glorious vestige. The sorcerer had informed him of his recent battle with the trio at the land of shadows. "But, my lord, they did not find the real sword, they would never hope to defeat you in truth. For it was merely an illusion. My lord, the Dreamcatchers of the haven are yours to command. Just one word from you and it would—"

"You repulsive swine! Your sympathy is as unwelcome as your

repugnant presence." The sorcerer's contemptuous words dripped with disdain as he spat in the face of the trembling subordinate. "I do not need your feeble attempts at assistance. I shall handle them myself," he declared, withdrawing from the quivering man, who recoiled from the noxious stench of the lord's breath.

With a menacing aura, the sorcerer continued, "They came closer than any in the past 500 years."

Resuming his pacing, the dark robes billowed dramatically behind him, giving the illusion of floating above the cold marble floor. He was truly a god among men and he would see to it becoming so.

These comparatively fragrant beings, though slightly less offensive to his senses, provided little solace for the agonizing and humiliating defeat he had recently suffered. As he turned to face them, his piercing gaze seemed to demand an explanation, silently urging the most intelligent among the pitiful lot to speak up.

The air hung heavy with the lord's displeasure—an oppressive atmosphere that left the room suffused with tension, as he awaited an explanation from the underlings who dared to fall short of his expectations.

"If I may, my lord," came a more confident voice beside the fat man. The slimmer figure patiently awaited the sorcerer's acknowledgement, which came in the form of a nod, granting him to speak.

This one knew the art of pleasing him, shown through the cultured tone that graced his words—a stark contrast to the unpleasantness that surrounded him. "Allow me to elucidate, my lord. A retired knight, a mere thief, and a lowly scoundrel. This pitiful trio stands no chance against the might of my lord. The scoundrel lacks the skill to wield a sword, as does the thief. The only formidable one remains—the

disgraced knight. This humble servant dares to suggest that, if it pleases my lord, the separation of this pathetic alliance may render their feeble powers to doom."

As the sorcerer paced about the marble floors, his disdain for bright colors evident, he had set loose gray shadows within the realm, transforming it to his somber taste. The subdued hues eased the strain on his black eyes, allowing him to navigate the realm with a certain satisfaction. The Dreamcatchers posed a formidable challenge for the trio, yet they proved insufficient, for the plans were no longer the same as when they had embarked on their journey.

The sorcerer's eyes darted around the realm and landed on the quivering elite—the four individuals cowering behind Baron and the plump one.

A sinister smile stretched across his face, beyond what seemed humanly possible, as an evil laughter escaped from his open maw. He reveled in the realization that Baron, despite being part of this quivering bunch, held a certain cunning that set him apart as the smartest. The sorcerer's gaze bore into Baron, a gleeful anticipation burning within his black eyes as he contemplated the twisted schemes that would unfold to bolster his insatiable hunger for power.

Defeated and disheartened, the trio slumped against the gnarled trunk of a colossal tree within the desolate expanse of the shadowlands. The real sword—the key to their quest—was now in the cunning hands of the sorcerer, his acting skills honed over the centuries he'd lived casting a shroud of uncertainty over their mission.

"Well," Frederick declared as he rose from his seat, determination etched across his features. "We can't stay here. I must train both of you. Ernest, you shall wield the sword, although your proficiency with daggers is noteworthy. We cannot predict when the sorcerer will strike, but we must be prepared to confront him head-on." A collective resolve marked their expressions, acknowledging the imminent danger that would descend upon them now that the sorcerer possessed the coveted sword.

There was a major flaw in their plan... they didn't have suitable training grounds. Reba, ever pragmatic, suggested, "We could return to the guardian. At least within the woods, we enjoyed safety for a while."

Agreeing quickly, the trio set out immediately, combining their journey with practice drills. The fake sword, though a mere replica, proved to be an effective training tool, with Frederick assuming that its proportions must mirror those of the real weapon.

Two days into their journey back to the guardian, Frederick urged Ernest to use the sword in combat. The transition from daggers to sword was tricky, yet Ernest tried his best, understanding that surrendering was no longer an option at this critical point.

The trio strategically decided on roles that aligned with their existing strengths—the men specializing in melee combat, while Reba would wield her bow and arrow for long-range attacks. Together, they confronted more formidable creatures of the shadow, surpassing the challenges posed by their previous encounters. Battles spanned entire days as the shadows grew stronger, hinting at the sorcerer's desperation.

Arriving at the edge of the land of shadows brought a momentary sigh of relief, quickly replaced by indignation, for they comprehended that their journey had only just begun. The sorcerer's forces would hunt them to no end. His defeat seemed to fuel his strength. The trio braced themselves for the relentless onslaught that awaited, their determination unwavering as they confronted the looming shadows of uncertainty and impending conflict.

This time, Ernest would sleep. He would train in his dreams as well, welding the power thereof. The sorcerer had centuries to perfect his craft, and Ernest refused to dwell on the massive power imbalance between them.

When they faced him in the tower, he could feel the same

helplessness he felt as a child. The memories of his mother's death haunted him still. It was hard not to feel like a child, for the lad certainly was greatly inexperienced in using the power of dreams to his advantage, leading him to stumble around like a maiden.

With every try, he would get more confident, but he needed guidance. Pearlie was long since under the control of the sorcerer. It would be a futile effort to have her teach him to navigate the vast realms safely.

Alas, they stood before the guardian's woods. The twisted woods were less menacing. It seemed like a field of daisies compared to the lands of the shadow. They faced the wolves again, stronger now, it was an easy defeat as the furs and leathers of the creatures were like butter compared to the tough skin and armor of some of the shadow creatures and illusions they'd faced.

The guardian's light emerged from within the woods. She easily understood that the sword they carried was a pale imitation left by the sorcerer. Anger welled up within her. The sorcerer will not win again, she reassured herself. Her eyes roamed the tired trio, wishing to ease their burden, but they must hurry. The holy power they'd harnessed briefly needed to be mastered should they hope to defeat him. Quickly, the guardian led them through the woods to the tower of their trials to the fairies.

The fairies, with delicate precision, wove a dome of divine light. This small yet enchanting sanctuary would serve as an ideal training ground for the trio. What made it even more extraordinary was the dome's manipulation of time—a secret the fairies eagerly shared. Within its confines, a mere day would pass in the outside world, while the trio could train for what felt like years.

Dumbfounded, the trio marveled at the intricate layers of divine light enveloping them. The dome resembled a tapestry of ethereal wings, streaked with veins of radiant brightness. As the light bathed them, a healing energy coursed through their bodies. Cuts and nicks from previous battles vanished within seconds, and even the claw wound Reba had sustained on her back healed seamlessly.

"The dome will sustain you," the fairies explained. "You will never hunger or tire, and your wounds will heal swiftly. Now, let us begin."

The trio, awestruck by the magical aura surrounding them, nodded in agreement. Setting aside their bags and cloaks, they assumed their fighting positions.

The guardian's smile radiated warmth as she gestured for the trio to sit. They settled on the ground, legs crossed before them, except for Reba, who leaned back on her palms. Frederick shot her a sharp look, prompting her to adjust her posture to mirror theirs. The guardian, with a face full of paternal concern, began to speak.

"I will teach you how to draw in the divided power. You must all learn to harness this power because, eventually, the sorcerer will confront you. He knows that your power is limited, but together, as a united force, you possess the strength to withstand him.

Now, I want you to close your eyes and remember the feeling you had when you made the shield. Tap into that feeling. Picture a well. Now, draw from that well with your will. Open your mind. Let all attachments fade away."

Ernest made the quickest progress, for he had no attachments to begin with—he was already alone and he recognized that it could be used as a strength for him.

Ernest could feel the warmth of the divine power welling up inside him. It burnt slightly but not so much as to make him uncomfortable. He felt it burned away all his insecurities, leaving him a different person, a better version of himself.

Reba watched as Ernest closed his eyes and began to glow softly. Frederick's face was scrunched up in concentration. Within her heart, she knew she would not access the well of power, for she knew she had too many attachments.

She did not like being alone. She did not want to be poor… she had many things that belonged to her, and she was not ready to let go of them.

The guardian looked at her knowingly. "I know you have many things for you to fear. Being without the things that you want makes you fearful. But I want you to know that those things are fleeting, they will fade away and they're just things. What you can only hope to be attached to are the hopes and dreams that those two have in you. For they believe that you can rise above what holds you down. They believe that you can rise above all. I believe that of you too."

Reba looked over at Frederick to see that he was glowing as well. She watched as Ernest fell backwards, but she knew he was fine.

She closed her eyes and focused on herself. She too would find the well and draw from the divine power. Ernest opened his eyes to find himself standing mysteriously above the city of Dream Haven.

The cloudless blue sky stretched above him, and he appeared to be standing on thin air. No wind stirred, no birds soared, and the city below seemed devoid of people. Before him, a figure materialized—a man with skin darkened by years in the sun, his long, dark hair pulled into a braid. He

donned silver armor with a sword strapped at his waist. Despite not knowing why, Ernest felt a familiarity with this man.

The man spoke in a soft voice, revealing the purpose of dreams. "Dreams are what the gods give humanity to find hope again amidst the darkness. No one should control them. No one should play God." The man then presented a crucial question to Ernest, "Will you use the power of dreams to destroy the evil that reigns terror over Dream Haven?"

The initial surprise had worn off from Ernest's face, replaced by determination. "Yes, I will," Ernest declared, prompting a nod from the man. In the man's outstretched hand, a small ball of light appeared.

Ernest opened his eyes to find himself standing somehow above the city of Dream Haven. A cloudless blue sky stretched above him and he seemed to be standing on thin air. There was no wind, no birds, nor were the people in the city below. A figure appeared in front of him. It was a man.

Ernest wondered who he was. Glancing at the sword on his hip emitting a soft hum, he was convinced it was the Sword of Forgotten Dreams. Ernest opened his mouth in surprise as he recognized the man before him as the Swordbearer.

His skin had been darkened by years in the sun. His long dark hair was pulled up in a braid and he didn't have silver armor with a sword strap at his waist. Ernest felt a sense of familiarity with this man, though he didn't know why.

The man spoke in a soft voice, "Dreams are what the gods use to give humanity hope—hope against the darkness that lies within every man. No one should control it. No one should play God. Ernest, will you use this power to destroy the creature that holds the dreams of many in his clutches?"

The Swordbearer looked at him with sad eyes. "The battle before will test your heart... the sword is the key. Protect it. Protect your company, for with them, your victory is sure. I will ask you again. Will you free the dreams in evil's hands?"

Tears gathered in the ancient hero's eyes as he remembered the pain of losing the sword. He wished to tell the young man that trust was very important. In his time, all hope was on his shoulders and he bore alone the heavy weight of the responsibility of keeping the peace and keeping evil at bay.

He wished to tell the young man how lucky he was to have friends who stood with him shoulder to shoulder, equal in strength. He was sure that he would realize it on his own, so he stayed silent.

The initial surprise had worn off Ernest's face. He faced this man with determination. "Yes, I will," Ernest said. The man nodded, and within his outstretched hand, lay a little ball of light.

Ernest opened his eyes to see Frederick lying on his back and Reba with her eyes closed, emitting a soft glow herself.

He looked over to the guardian. "How much time has passed?"

She stared at the lad with a smile. "These visions take years, sometimes decades to finish for the trance you just left took you three moons, mastering the power would take even longer, so we must begin. We cannot wait for your friends to join us in due time."

Frederick opened his eyes to see his old master. His master, despite his age, was a large muscular man with a long gray beard. His stern but kind eyes and facial scars spoke a great deal of his battle experience. They stood in what appeared to be the training ground of the knight academy.

"Step forward, young knight," he said. "Before you lies a path many would not dare take." He paused, letting the weight of these utterances sink in. "Is your shield merely for decoration, or are your calluses merely for stories?" the elder bellowed.

"No, master!" the knight declared with resolve.

"The weight is heavy, but will you take it?" the elderly knight pressed further. "Yes, I will master it."

The old knight stretched out his hand, and within it lay a small glowing ball. Frederick's eyes fluttered open.

The trance slightly disorienting him. He felt a hand on his shoulder lifting him up. Ernest's eyes shone with newfound wisdom. "Welcome back, Fred," he said, patting him on the back. Eyes darting around, he spotted Reba's frame on the floor a few feet away. Her body was emitting a soft glow.

Ernest's voice snapped him out of his momentary daze. "Are you ready?" Frederick smiled in response.

Before Reba stood her old teacher. The wispy man taught her all she knew about how to survive as a thief. The man's face, usually in a permanent smirk, was now serious… for she knew this man was not her teacher. Aba was his name.

"You have been taught to steal, you have been taught to survive, but you have not been taught to fight. For this teacher of yours has failed you. Nonetheless, you must choose."

"I did what I had to do to survive. I do not blame Aba. I love you like a father." The eyes of her teacher lit up in a smile.

"Instead of survival, will you live just this once? Will you live not for yourself but for many others who do not know you? Will you live knowing that you may lose your life in pursuit of heroism?"

"Yes, I will, teacher," Reba said with resolution. A familiar smile stretched the old man's face. A shiny golden ball floated in his outstretched hand.

Her eyes opened to find the men engaged in a brawl. But instead of their usual weapons, Ernest had disposed of his knives and in place of them was a blade of light, almost half as tall as he was. Frederick similarly had a large blade of light that bore a resemblance to his broad sword.

"Welcome back," said the soothing voice of a fairy.

"They've been acting for the past few months now." Reba remembered that a year within the dome was similar to an hour outside. Her training would just begin. It was noon in Dream Haven. The sun would hang high, shining her glorious beings down to the inhabitants of Dream Haven as per usual.

Today, however, those who were outside went about business as usual but added some more spring in their steps to hasten before the storm arrived.

The guardian stepped to the edge of a cliff overlooking Dream Haven. She sensed it first before she saw it. Her heart thumped faster within her chest. The sorcerer had started with his spell. She recalled the last time he did it because she was barely a century old. Young by her people's standards. She remembered the heavy feeling of dread that filled her then. Her feet told her to flee from the malevolent magic.

Stealing her heart and raising her head. She stood firm and channeled her divine power to a small part of the woods. It was where the heroes trained. Telling them of the impending prophecy of doom would have to wait. It would only distract them from their current trial. When they were ready, she renewed hope in herself with this small chant.

An old woman stopped mid-step to look at the sky. She sensed magic. Powerful magic, but being common, there was nothing she could do. She sensed a great evil in that magic that would do nothing but much harm. She hastened to her home… toward her son. Edin did not listen to her as usual, but instead, he pleaded with her to keep her voice lower lest the Dreamcatchers would hear her to find them. But it was too late.

CHAPTER 13

BLADES OF LIGHT

Her son shook his head. "Mother, do you remember what happened the last time someone spoke of magic and dreams in front of the Dreamcatchers?" he said quietly, gripping his wife's hand.

"Please keep your voice down and do not bring doom upon our family. But you know..." She trailed off as a strange purple glow filled the room—it was too late... the spell had been cast. The woman turned to look at her family and saw that her son, his wife, and their two children were all asleep.

Marine pushed open the door to their small house and found that the streets were littered with sleeping people. In the distance, she could see Dreamcatchers and soldiers marching down the street in various formations.

The Dreamcatcher at the helm of the formation observed the old woman in front of a small house. Her eyes were wide open. 'She must be a dreamer,' he thought to himself. Dreamers were the only ones who could withstand the spell of the dark lord. 'Not for long,' he thought. Soon, they would fall. All would fall before the dark lord's spell. All would worship him as the new God of Dreams.

The necklace their commander handed out to them glowed in resistance to the weaves of the spell. They were told that it would protect them from its control. The Dreamcatcher wondered how life would be when he would be a captain in the armies of the new God of Dreams. He gave a sinister smile beneath his helmet.

Baron looked out the window, observing the serenity in the city below.

Rows of Dreamcatchers prowled the city in an orderly manner. Being in charge of their training, he was proud of their orderliness. His peace was ruined by the loud breathing of Gregor beside him.

"A-are you sure w-we are safe?" the short man asked, fiddling with the emerald jewel pendant hanging on his neck.

"Our lord has promised us we will be safe. Now, stop your whining." The lanky elite walked briskly away from the window, passing Edwin. 'That strange idiot,' he thought to himself.

He soon heard the heavy steps of Gregor's fat little legs chasing him. "Wait!" the stubby man yelled. Paying him no mind, the slim noble opened the double doors to his study. The plush carpet silencing the loud cracks of his heeled boots against the floor.

Gregor's heavy pants filled the room as Baron poured himself a glass of well-aged wine. Gregor waddled to the sofa before the room's great window. Baron gracefully sat behind his great dark wood desk. Gregor's voice snapped him out of the blissful silence.

"Repeat that," he said.

"I said, aren't you worried about the common folk? They've been standing as statues for the past two days!" Baron did not care much for the common folk, he barely considered them at all. Gregor, however, found them charming. He had many servants and sometimes allowed them into his dreamscape without the knowledge of the Dreamcatchers.

Baron propped his feet on the edge of his table, disinterested in the conversation. 'Gregor will eventually tire,' he thought to himself.

His mind went to the weeks leading up to this day. Members of the great hall had accused him of his authority over the Dreamcatchers. They said his methods were too heavy on the common folk. They laid accusations of dictatorship against him.

He remembered Atlanta, one of the elders. Her cold and calculative eyes raked over him and his cohorts. He knew she was behind it as he had received word from his informants. They told him that people were asking questions. He also spotted a few oddities around his place in the dreamscapes. He was sure she had been onto him and she didn't hide her complete disdain for him.

'None of that matters,' he thought with a sinister smile that mirrored his lord's. She was a strong dreamer, but she would not be able to withstand his might. The city would soon be in ruin. Nightmares and shadow creatures had taken habitation there. His Dreamcatchers patrolled the city. All was going well.

It took all of Marine's willpower to stay awake but she knew it was futile. She had heard stories about this Dark Lord from her father when she was young—he was a great old sorcerer who had plunged the world into ruin millennia ago, although she thought he was dead now. In one last attempt to stay awake, she made a silent prayer to the gods to send help.

A Dreamcatcher tripped on something while those ahead of him found more sleeping bodies. Some stumbled out into open streets looking dazed while others tried to run, only to fall asleep yards away from where they started.

Soon, the spell of the sorcerer would be complete and the common folk would be under his control. They were protected because they had a long, simple sworn alliance with the mighty sorcerer. They were smart enough to see that the sorcerer was the most powerful being to ever exist. The gods would not be sending anyone or anything their way. The world belonged to them now.

The guardian stood outside the dome, feeling a strong breeze carrying a gust of the sorcerer's magic through it all around her. She remembered how before war broke out between humans and shadows, fairies roamed free throughout lands, but after the war destroyed much of the world, only a handful of them were left scattered across different parts of the world fighting against extinction.

The only fairies left inhabited the tower now. The sorcerer had pushed them to the brink, being fearful of the fact that they were conduits of divine power bestowed by the gods themselves. But now he would control all, should the training heroes fail.

And elves were reduced from millions strong to a selfish thousand. The dwarves had permanently secluded themselves into the great mines that were within caverns of mountains, bearing scars of the battles, and the dryads were reduced to a handful.

During the last war, all the species banded together to stop him, led by the Swordbearer. Now, only three stood before him in opposition. She did not want to feel pessimistic, but the odds were not in their favor. She looked back in the direction of the dome. Perhaps it was time to intensify their efforts.

He had corrupted everything in his wake to control life and death, feasting on the powers of dreams. She wondered what else he would strive for after the destruction of the world as he walked back to the tower. It wouldn't be long now before his power covered the woods.

Marine woke up suddenly with gray eyes, taking everything in sight around her—still in Dream Haven, but this version lacked any color or vibrance. Its inhabitants walked around with blank white eyes while elites mingled among poorer folks without any discrimination whatsoever. It made no sense at all!

She frantically searched for Edin, her son, until finally spotting him meters ahead, then hastened steps towards catching up and quickly pulling on his shoulder, asking, "What is wrong with you? Where is my grandchild? Where is your wife?" Her voice rose louder with each word until, suddenly, powerful hands of dark magic pulled Marine back into slumber once again.

Baron watched safely from inside the mansion's third-story window, yet the sweaty elite next to him irked Baron deeply. "Would you stop trembling!" he spat at Gregor. Irritably adding, "The Dark lord assured us we are safe."

Noisy trembling ceased briefly, warranting a sigh by Baron walking briskly off, saying nothing more than reminding Gregor how things had changed within Dream Haven since joining forces with the sorcerer, who had brought change everywhere except for those who were too proud to lower themselves before his greatness.

"Do you recall Bexley?" Baron inquired of Gregor. "Yes. What about him?"

"Exactly!" yelled Baron. "He's not here with us. He dared to speak against our lord saying that no one would be so powerful as to reign such terror upon the world, and now look at him. He's mingling with the common folk. Which will be your fate if you continue to irk me!" he spat, earning a grimace from Gregor.

Gregor stayed silent this time. The weight of the threat hung heavily in the air. Baron was the closest to the dark lord. He would do well not to irk him.

Gregor knew all too well how insane Baron was. He recalled one time when they were much younger. Baron and he were fishing for pearls within dreamscapes when the son of Edinburgh came to them with his company of bullies.

They had come to steal their find. Pearls within the dreamscapes would be sold for much once they were made real with magic. His father owned the territory where they were plenty.

Edinburgh did not respect this. He coveted the pearls and would sometimes send his machinations to disrupt the fishing process. This time, his burly son, Edward showed up. Gregor remembered being beaten up and left alone after that. Baron, on the other hand, had decided he would rip apart the Edinburghs for what they did.

In the months following that, Baron laid steep accusations against them. From corruption to rape and even murder. They were found guilty. Baron didn't just stop there. He made sure every last one of them died at his hands. He set nightmares on them within the dreamscapes. It didn't matter that they begged for mercy. Baron was just that wicked.

It was no wonder that when they were approached by the sorcerer's agent, he easily accepted the proposal. Baron loved to watch people suffer. He loved to control all. The sorcerer had promised him Dream Haven as well as a large and profitable portion of dreamscapes.

Baron was simply ecstatic with that development.

The city was now a den of monsters. They freely destroyed houses, completely oblivious as to the differences between mansions and huts. The streets were littered with concrete and wood—the rubble of the once great city of Dream Haven. Every now and then, Dreamcatchers would Patrol a given street.

Not caring as much about whether they found one or two people awake, they would soon become slaves for the dark one's army.

Marine had been in hiding for the past day in different houses. Sometimes she would feel the black tendrils of the sorcerer's power tugging at her soul. The only option was to stay away being that it kept most of the power at bay. She hoped to find others like her, but every time she saw them, her eyes would catch one or two nightmares around.

She could not face the nightmares. Obviously, she was too weak to do that. She silently prayed to the God of dreams to send help. She would huddle in and out of stalls, stealing food and moving as fast as her old feet could take her.

More than the exhaustion she felt, she was sleepy and just wanted to doze off for an hour or two to recuperate her strength, but she knew it was not possible, otherwise, she would fall into the zombie- like state of others.

Sometimes the nightmares saw her but chose to ignore her—perhaps they thought she was too weak to do anything. She couldn't help but agree with them, after all, what would a woman of 84 years be able to do?

She walked slowly, leaning on her stick to a shop that was halfway standing and the other half destroyed. She remembered she used to walk by this shop years past. The shop sold food and canned items that were beyond what her short pocket could afford most of the time. This time, she walked into the shop, being careful of the large lumps of concrete and wood that lay about it.

She picked up a couple of things here and there—just enough to survive for the next couple of days. She grabbed bottles of water and a blanket, hoping somehow that help would come, but if it didn't, she didn't know how long she would survive. She silently prayed to see another person. If the destruction of the city did not kill her, the sheer loneliness would.

Atlanta staggered slowly, putting one foot in front of the other. The city had long since fallen to ruin. Many moons ago, Baron tried to convince her to join his group. She never felt an affinity towards them. Baron and Gregor alone possessed control over the Dreamcatchers, which was enough reason to keep away from them.

She always thought Baron's eyes betrayed pride and madness. The man also hated the common folk and it was in his time as commander of the Dreamcatchers that the sudden segregation of the common folk from the elite became more pronounced. He also started to take away many common things that happened to be dreamers.

She found him too suspicious, so she and a few other strong elites launched a discreet inquiry as to Baron's affairs. And last month, they struck gold. They made a discovery that he, along with many other notable elite, were in cohorts with the sorcerer.

Now, many among the elite said amongst themselves that the sorcerer was just an old wife's tale. Nothing but an old folklore told by mothers to scare their children. Nothing of import. It didn't matter anymore. The sorcerer lived and he had control over most of the city.

Atlanta spotted a gray head ducking behind a wall. 'A dreamer,' she thought. 'A powerful one at that.' She silently limped over to the frail form in a beige threadbare frock. The woman looked up, recognition shining in her tired eyes.

"Are there others like you?" Marine inquired of her. Atlanta began to recount her experiences. She didn't know from when—all she knew was that the older woman made her feel safe.

The old woman held bags of food, bottles of water, and a large blanket. She leaned on a stick to walk.

She helped her to her feet, eyes scanning for a building still standing to serve as a hideout. Atlanta spoke of the discoveries made from her investigations into Baron. Her recount earned a soft grasp from the feeble woman beside her. Her eyes widened in disbelief and surprise. It didn't seem so far- fetched now. Skepticism would help no one. They could only hope together and silently for help to come.

Ernest leaped, dodging Frederick's broad sword swing, easily visible over the past few months of training together within the dome. Their faces shone youthfully despite the passage of time, due perhaps to the magical aura surrounding them, slowing the aging process somewhat.

Ernest especially showed significant growth, sporting lean muscles covering a taller frame, twice the hair length even though cutting regularly never seemed enough, confusing Frederick greatly.

The guardian judged Ernest to be the strongest in the group, making the most progress. Shielding themselves within the dreamscapes was a difficult task considering that the sorcerer was the strongest within the realm.

Reba had learned to conjure up a mythical bow using divine power. The bow would string itself once she pulled back the drawstring. Releasing it would fire an arrow made of divine power, strong enough to cause an explosion. But she was to use the bow as her last resort against the sorcerer. Instead, she would fire from a magical crossbow that always armed itself.

"You have done well," said the familiar voice of the guardian. She stepped lightly with bare feet towards the trio. "It is time for the next phase of your training," she added with a comforting smile on her face. Together, they willed their weapons away and sat cross-legged, except for Reba, once again. This time, Frederick conjured a small ball of divine power and flung it at her, hitting her arms and causing her to fall. The fall earned a pleasant laughter from all of them.

The laughter faded away to Reba's disgruntled voice. "How many more phases are left this time?"

The guardian glanced at her. "It is time to learn how to dreamwalk. Ernest can already do it. But the rest of you can't. Dreamwalking does not need sleep to operate. You will be wide awake but slipping between the fabric of what lays awake and what does not. This is how the sorcerer moves from one place to the next in the twinkle of an eye," she said with a snap of her fingers, meeting their eyes one after the other.

For the next year, the trio learned to dreamwalk under the direct supervision of the guardian herself.

Ernest jumped out of the dreamscape with a startled yelp, calling the attention of the others. His face was a mask of rage. "Did you know?!" he directed at the guardian. Frederick and Reba, confused, darted their eyes back and forth between the duo.

"Yes. I did," she said silently. "You are not ready," she quickly added, watching Ernest pace the length of the dome.

"Any day, any time," said Frederick, prompting Reba to nod in agreement. "Know what?" she pressed.

Ernest looked too angry to speak as he paced, mumbling incoherent words at the dome, leaving the guardian to tell them what was happening in Dream Haven at that moment. With each passing word, their faces fell and then morphed into masks of pain and anger.

"I kept this from you knowing fully well you are not ready. You still aren't. You are at but a fraction of the level you need to be in order to defeat the sorcerer." She stopped, letting her words sink in. Ernest collapsed onto the grass of the clearing. He knew she was right. The little he saw scared him to his bones.

He hardened his resolve. "What more do we need to know?" he asked with determination.

The guardian looked at them, unsurprised at their resolve.

She remembered when they first came to the Whispering Woods to find the sword. Ernest, unsure but resilient, now met her gaze with determination and inner strength; Reba, always avoiding confrontation, cunning and slippery, was now finding her courage and learned to trust her companions, and Frederick, the disgraced knight carrying a chip on his back, never fully reconciling with his past, now stood with his head held high.

She smiled. "I will tell you once you have mastered the dreamwalk."

The trio were impatient. The guardian assured them of the time difference within the dome. They relaxed slightly into their dreamwalk pose, standing in a natural position with their legs shoulder-width apart. The way was to induce sleep and then shroud their souls with divine power. This would, in turn, warp their bodies into the dream realm.

It took months, but they all succeeded.

They also learned how to shroud themselves with divine power as an aura. The shield would protect them from being detected in the dreamscapes.

In those months, the group found it difficult to cover much distance within the dreamscapes using the dreamwalk. Frederick, especially, found it most difficult. This was because he never had the affinity to dream in the first place… or so he thought.

They were able to resolve this problem as the guardian told

Frederick that dreaming was not a talent but simply a way of life. She explained that the act of dreaming was tied to hope. Frederick could easily relate to hope. It was, along with faith, honor, and valor, a key tenant of the code of knighthood. Knowing this, he was soon able to join his companions in progress.

Ernest could also feel the gentle tug of the sword as he grew stronger. He could feel it calling out to him. His mind raced with the possibilities of how to kill the sorcerer. He would soon discover that the sorcerer could only be killed by divine power or the sword, which was made from divine power.

The sword was apparently forged by the dwarves using divine power along with the fairies using a rare metal. He thought that perhaps infusing the sword with divine power or turning the sword into a blade of light would end the sorcerer once and for all.

Ernest told the guardian of his plan, which she greatly endorsed. She thought that it would seem the heroes were maybe just the ones to end the reign of terror. Hope was rekindled in her heart as she watched the quick growth of the trio. She now rest assured that they could vanquish evil before them, and most importantly, stay alive.

"The sorcerer will cover the world with his magic once again. It will turn that breath into his slaves as he harvests their souls in the dreamscape." She further told them of the aftermath of the last great war. She told them of her own deepest fears that it would happen again if they failed in their quest.

CHAPTER 14

THE FINAL PARRY

The heroes looked grimly at the words of the guardian. "Well, I guess we have to wrap this up then," Reba said, breaking through the silence, causing a chuckle from Frederick. He was the first to get up, followed by Ernest. Their spirits were light but the journey was grim.

'We might just make it,' Ernest thought to himself. The years he spent within the dome filled him with much-needed wisdom for the coming battle.

He knew they were not ready yet, but they would make it. According to the guardian, nightmares surrounded Dream Haven on all sides, leaving their entrance a mystery. To that end, Reba shared an idea for using her newfound abilities to which Frederick vehemently opposed. "That's too dangerous. If the fall doesn't kill us first, the buildings will," he said with a smirk on his face, which did little to hide his excitement.

"Well, I guess we'll have to find out then," Ernest said with a smile. He looked over at the fairy beside him. The little creature gave him a smile.

"Be careful," she said. "Bring the sword back to us in one piece, and yourself," she added. "Us, yes... the sword, not so much," Frederick said with a chuckle.

Ernest gazed up at him, shaking his head as he turned back to the fairy. "We will try. It feels good to know that you care for our safety."

"Of course," came the soft voice of the guardian. "You are our heroes," she said.

The armor the guardian gave them was made with divine power, so it would shield them from direct attacks from the shadow creatures and the nightmares.

The most worry she had, however, was for the stronger elite that were under the thrall of the sorcerer. She could not gauge their power, for many of them had spent years residing in the dreamscapes, molding it into their versions of perfection. When they put on their armor, she looked at them and her gentle smile fell.

"Be careful," she began. "I know you have heard me say this many times, but know that you have strength together. Together, you will defeat the evil of the sorcerer. Together, you will end his reign of terror for good. But remember that your very strength is your weakness and he will try to separate you and pick you off one by one. Do not forget your training, always remember the decades you spent within this dome. You have grown in wisdom, you have grown in strength, you have grown in character and I couldn't be more proud. I am certain that you will be victorious."

The guardian laid a hand on each of their shoulders, blessing them, gently nodding her head, and with all that done, she sent them off.

The guardian watched the trios' backs as they ran in the direction of Dream Haven. The sorcerer's magic was only stronger in the air now as she could almost taste it—the fairies had retreated into the tower and so did she, for the magic that had long since covered the Whispering Woods would soon turn the once peaceful forest into another land of shadows.

Thinking of the guardian's revelation to them, the air was heavy, tasting of their impending doom.

The valiant heroes raced with a swiftness that surpassed even the speed of horses. Their goal was to reach Dream Haven and release its innocent inhabitants from the clutches of terror.

Ernest's mind was flooded with visions of Dream Haven within the dreamscapes. It appeared as though the sorcerer had extended his black inky tendrils, which he used against them, all over Dream Haven.

These tendrils were inside everyone's mouths, or so it seemed at first glance. Upon further reflection, however, Ernest realized that there were a few other dreamers who could resist the snakes of the sorcerer's power just like him.

He conjectured that this might be due to the fact that the sorcerer had stretched his powers too thin and far.

Reba looked perplexed as they spoke about this matter, but Ernest continued on unabatedly, "There are some within the citadel who remain untouched by the sorcerer's power... I do not think it is their choice."

Reba stared at him incredulously. "You mean...?" she asked Ernest. "Yes," he replied grimly.

Reba offered her services without hesitation. "Let me take care of them first! They will never see arrows coming."

Frederick nodded in agreement. "You can have them if you want."

As they approached the Great City from afar, they witnessed hordes of nightmares and shadow creatures surrounding the high walls around it.

"Are we still doing this?" Reba asked hesitantly.

"Why not?" responded Ernest confidently, earning a scowl from Frederick.

According to the plan, Frederick hurled both Reba and Ernest into the skies while he launched himself using a longsword made out of divine power vaulting into the sky above the city gates.

Their landing caused Frederick to scream uncontrollably until the creatures below frantically searched for the source, finally spotting a small trail composed entirely of divine light shaped like an arrowhead heading straight towards the southern gate, where the entire horde gathered.

Arrows struck the ground, obliterating everything near wooden doors, leaving a gaping hole behind. "Oops!" exclaimed Reba nonchalantly, shrugging her shoulders slightly. They landed before the broken gate, having only seconds before being overwhelmed by waiting monsters.

They quickly assessed their surroundings and then ran into the city, meeting multitudes fleeing through the streets. It became clear after mere moments that these people had been trapped here for days on end without any hope left whatsoever. The people were locked in a trance just as the guardian had told them. Unsure of what to do, Ernest took a step approaching the still multitude, followed by Frederick and Reba.

Sensing no danger, Ernest picked up the pace resuming his run, and so did the rest. He purposely stayed as close to the wall as possible to avoid provoking a reaction from the otherwise still crowd.

Then, all of a sudden, the nearest man ran towards him, a snarl on his face and his hand stretched out in front of him. From then, chaos commenced and the massive crowd before them started to chase.

"Above you!" Frederick shouted. Ernest's eyes caught sight of a shadow monster and then two crawling over the walls, spotting him.

They would fight on two fronts, it seemed. They were prepared. The battle raged with the heroes mostly killing the monsters but only slightly injuring the people and rendering them incapable of moving. But it did not stop them. It only seemed to slow them down. They would only stop when the sorcerer was defeated.

Reba yielded over the sound of snarls and roars. "Then we must move," Frederick said. "We cannot delay here." Frederick took Reba by the arm and up into the air. With a squeal, she landed upon the nearest building—a two-story shop.

She climbed onto the roof and gave a signal, signifying a clear road ahead. Ernest leaped to meet her, leaving Frederick to charge his way through the nylon crowd. They moved, hopping from roof to roof, making their way to the city center. They covered much ground, leaping on the roof they were just about to leave, worried by another crowd coming from the west.

They headed north and then back again to the remaining course, hoping to outrun the crowd and the monsters running beside them. It became clear that to cover much ground, they must dreamwalk, and so they did.

They knew, however, that entering into the dreamscapes would only alert the sorcerer of their exact whereabouts. But they did it regardless. Just before Frederick was about to leap, he was grabbed by the foot and tossed several hundred feet into the air by a large shadow spider.

Landing with a frown on his face, he brandished his broadsword, a blade forged from divine light that gleamed with celestial brilliance, casting an ethereal glow against his face. The ominous silhouette of a 30-foot shadow spider sized him up, its eight legs skittering eerily across the city.

Around him, the air seemed to thicken as nightmare wolves came at him from the shadows, their glowing eyes fixated on Frederick, whispering at him to take a nap. The zombie-like figures—the fastest runners of the cursed people of Dream Haven —shuffled towards him with relentless determination.

With a resolute gaze, Frederick faced the looming threat. The divine light of his broadsword flickered, casting an ethereal glow that banished the encroaching darkness. The shadow spider, a creature born of the abyss, lunged at him with wicked intent. Frederick's swift reflexes allowed him to parry the monstrous arachnid's attacks, each clash of blades resonating with the clash of opposing forces.

As the battle unfolded, nightmare wolves circled, their haunting howls reverberating through the crowded street. Frederick, with his divine broadsword, deftly struck down the nightmare wolves one by one, the celestial light dispelling the nightmares they carried. His movements were a dance of precision, an intricate choreography of offense and defense.

Amidst the relentless onslaught, the crowd closed in. Frederick's broadsword carved through the puppet horde with otherworldly grace, its divine light purging the cursed existence that animated them.

The celestial brilliance of the sword illuminated the grim faces of the zombie-like creatures, revealing the tragic remnants of their lives.

The shadow spider intensified its assault. Frederick, however, stood unwavering, channeling the divine power within his broadsword. With a powerful swing, he struck the creature, the radiant light searing through the shadows that comprised its form. The shadow spider recoiled, its dark essence recoiling from the divine onslaught.

As the battlefield quieted, Frederick surveyed the aftermath. The divine light of his broadsword dimmed as he channeled it away. The 30-foot shadow spider, its once formidable presence diminished, dissipated into the abyss. Frederick's dream leaped to catch up with his companions. He hoped they were not separated as his form disappeared.

He reappeared before the great hall. The sounds of the battle within hurting his steps, which echoed in the haunting silence of the corridor.

Suddenly, he paused, catching a moving figure with his left eye. It was an elderly woman running from a shadow monster. She appeared to be in good health. Most likely the others that Ernest mentioned. Wasting no time. He brandished his broadsword, leaping high into the air as he readied for a downward slash. The woman, seeing his intentions, slid in his direction. He fell, slicing the shadow monster through the middle. He turned to look at the woman. Her calculative eyes roamed his form, assessing whether he was friend or foe.

He found no offense in her actions. He was preparing to attack the other creatures that came after.

He fought for what seemed like an eternity, the wave of nightmares and shadow creatures exhausted. He looked at the woman. His eyes taking in her fanciful yet torn frock. 'A symbol of nobility,' he thought to himself. She was about to speak when he raised his hand to silence her. Her wise eyes shining in defiance.

"Run. Hide. This is no place for you. Only come out when you cannot feel his power." His tone did not warrant any sort of response. Still, she raised her head in a final act of defiance, nodded in acknowledgment, and ran off.

The great hall stood before them, guarded by formidable elite Dreamcatchers, their shadows pulsating with malevolent energy. Ernest, the hero, brandished his divine light sword, its ethereal glow casting an otherworldly luminescence across the dim chamber.

Beside him, Reba, the skilled archer, notched an arrow onto her mythical bow, her steely gaze fixed on the advancing Dreamcatchers.

Ernest and Reba blinked to the front of the great hall, before which stood a squadron of Dreamcatchers.

As the first wave lunged forward, Ernest moved with preternatural grace, his sword slashing through the soldiers. Each swing carved a path of radiant destruction, dispelling the dark magic that fueled the Dreamcatchers. The divine light emitted by his sword illuminated the hall, revealing intricate patterns etched into the walls—an eerie tapestry of dreams and nightmares.

Reba, positioned strategically, unleashed a volley of arrows with unparalleled precision. Her mythical bow hummed with ancient power, each arrow finding its mark with unerring accuracy.

The Dreamcatchers, though formidable, faltered under the relentless assault. The combination of divine light and mythical arrows created a dance of destruction, weaving through the shadows that sought to protect the great hall and their master within.

The elite Dreamcatchers, recognizing the threat, intensified their efforts. Shadows coiled around them like vipers, forming a shield against the heroes. A new power granted by the sorcerer no less.

Ernest thought to himself, 'They couldn't do that when I last saw them.' Undeterred, he summoned the power within his sword, unleashing a radiant shockwave that shattered the shadowy defense.

The great hall echoed with the clash of divine forces and malevolent agents. Reba, nimble and agile, danced between the swirling darkness, her bowstring singing as she continued her relentless barrage.

Each arrow made with ancient magic found its mark, weakening the Dreamcatchers one by one. Yet, the elite guardians fought fiercely, their shadowy tendrils reaching out to ensnare the heroes.

Ernest, sensing the growing peril, called upon the divine energy coursing through his sword of light. The blade intensified, emitting a blinding radiance that dispelled the encroaching shadows.

With a resolute cry, he surged forward, cleaving through the Dreamcatchers with unmatched strength. His every strike was a testament to the mastery he had gained within the divine dome.

Reba's perceptiveness altered her strategy. She aimed for the heart of each of the Dreamcatchers, exploiting weaknesses exposed by Ernest's divine onslaught.

Her arrows, infused with the essence of her mythical bow, pierced through the darkness, further debilitating the Dreamcatchers. The great hall, once shrouded in shadow, now bore witness to a clash of extraordinary forces.

The divine light and mythical prowess of Ernest and Reba harmonized, creating a symphony of destruction that reverberated through the chamber.

The Dreamcatchers, their strength waning, fought desperately to protect the great enemy lurking within the hall. In a final surge of power, Ernest and Reba synchronized their attacks.

The divine light merged with the mythical energy, creating a radiant storm that engulfed the remaining elite Dreamcatchers. The shadows recoiled, unable to withstand the combined might of the hero and archer.

As the last Dreamcatcher dissolved into dissipating shadows, the great hall stood liberated. Ernest, his divine light sword gleaming, and Reba, her mythical bow at rest, shared a moment of triumphant silence. The great enemy awaited, the culmination of their arduous journey drawing near.

"Looks like I missed the party." Frederick's voice rumbled behind them. He looked worn and torn but otherwise fine.

They shared a quick embrace, relieved to see him in one piece. He recalled his encounter with the spicy old woman, who Reba had named "Spicy" because of her salt and pepper hair.

The heroes, now complete, shared one more laugh before they faced the end of this journey. Together, they walked into the deeper parts of the hall where the magic of the sorcerer was thickest. Atlanta hurried to the hideout. She could barely wait to tell them what she had witnessed.

"We're saved," she informed the group. She went further to recount the experience with the tall strangely armored knight. The armor was unlike any other she had ever seen. It seemed to be most delicately sewn leather with curved plates of a strange dark silver metal. It was no work of any blacksmith of Dream Haven.

She went into full detail about what he said. She encouraged them to act with fate, then with her words. They made plans on how they would help the strange elf. She encouraged her mates to capture Baron

and his cohorts once the sorcerer was defeated. With Marine agreeing with her, the other members of the group of eight had no choice. They first needed to secure rope.

CHAPTER 15

THE ILLUSION'S EMBRACE

The air in Dream Haven had an unsettling stillness as if the very fabric of reality had been woven with threads of deception. The trio of heroes—Ernest, Reba, and Frederick—found themselves stepping deeper into the basement of the great hall. They shared a knowing look. It was time to take a dreamwalk. They soon found themselves facing the sorcerer, who, despite initial appearances, wielded an immense power they had underestimated.

In an unexpected surge of magical prowess, the sorcerer cast a potent spell, unraveling the unity that had bound the three friends together. They were scattered like leaves in the wind, each transported to a dreamscape tailored to their deepest desires.

ERNEST'S DREAM: THE DANCE OF SHADOWS AND A FORGOTTEN PAST

Ernest found himself in a realm of perpetual twilight where shadows danced in harmony with his every move. The enchanting whispers of the shadows promised him the life he'd always yearned for—a world where he was the undisputed master of his destiny. Here, he reveled in the thrill of his victories, basking in the admiration of an adoring crowd. Yet, beneath the surface, a gnawing emptiness lingered, questioning the authenticity of this apparent triumph.

The scene changed, showing his small home. The one he shared with his beloved mother. He was back in his childhood again. The reality dawned on him as he ran to the door.

Pushing the frail wooden plank open, his mother stood up with a worried look on her face before morphing into anger.

"Ernest! How many times must I tell you to never come home past sundown!?" his mother said while dragging him by the arm. Ernest heard nothing. He hugged his mother with all the might in that little body of his. Soon after, her arms snaked around him, causing sobs to rack his small body.

"My sweet boy. Who hurt you? Was it Bern? Talk to me." She pulled out of his embrace to look at her son. He was acting strange. She checked him for bruises as it wouldn't be the first time he would come home with them.

Ernest was home.

The next morning, Ernest woke up with a huge smile on his young face. He leaped from the bed to find his mother.

"Mother! I saw something yesterday," young Ernest said to his mom as she made dinner, but she wasn't paying much attention to him. She was lost in her thoughts, remembering what had happened in the marketplace earlier in the day. Regardless, he didn't stop. He went on to tell her what he had seen.

"There was a horse, and I was walking in a beautiful place. Everything was bright and pretty like the flowers at the palace gates. Mom, are you listening?" He tugged on her dress and finally got her attention.

"Oh, son. Yes, I am listening. What were you saying again?" she asked, this time, paying more attention to him.

Smiling, Ernest continued with his story. "Then I saw a bright light from the middle of the woods. It looked like it was the source of the other light."

Ylva, Ernest's mom, was confused. Where had he seen what he was talking about? It wasn't as though they had gone anywhere the day before. However, she kept listening. Perhaps it was something from his imagination. Kids could be so silly at times.

"Okay. So, what happened to the light?" Ylva asked, smiling at him. "Did you see the source?"

"No. It wasn't a light. It was a big knife… like what the guards carry around." Ernest was trying to remember what it was called, and he tilted his head to the side. "Don't say it, Mom. I will remember the name," he assured her.

Ylva smiled. Ernest was her bundle of joy, and she couldn't imagine life without him. He was the best gift life had given her.

Ernest stopped himself. He had been in this moment before. If he spoke of the dream, his mother would get killed. He would not lose her again.

"Ernest? Keep going," she urged in a soft voice.

"It was nothing, Mother. I'm just joking. I saw nothing," the boy said with a smile.

"Well, if you do see something, tell no one or the Dreamcatchers will find you." Ylva caressed her son's cheek with a stern look on her face. She would not risk losing her sweet boy.

Five winters later, Ernest bid his mother goodbye as he walked out of their small wooden home. He bounced in his step as he approached the forked road meters away. Arms pulled him into a harsh embrace as Bern and Carl pulled him to themselves. The teens chatted happily, making their way to the pier where they would listen to Old Man Tarren tell his tales.

They had kept the ritual every day for the past years, and today was no different. Ernest paused mid- step. His eyes moved to a dream merchant. He knew her. Her name was Pearlie and she gave him a map. Realizing where he was, he ran back to his mother to say goodbye one last time.

Ylva peered up in confusion as her son barged into the house. With tears in his eyes, he pulled her into an embrace, sobbing. Ylva stayed silent, waiting for her son to speak.

"I love you, Mother. But this is not real." Slowly, the dream unraveled. He clutched the form of his mother tighter, not wanting to let go.

"Let me go, my son," Ylva said gently. "These past few years have been the best of my life. I had a chance with you."

She reached up to caress his tear-stained cheek. "The world needs you to be brave. I need you to be brave. You can do that, yes?" Her sweet voice cracked at the end. Tears welled up in her eyes as she gazed longingly at her son. He nodded. Ernest's eyes flew open. He was in the land of shadows again. He was not lost. For he would find his friends.

REBA'S DREAM: THE VAULT OF RICHES AND THE PROMISES OF A PARENT

Reba, in her dream, stood within an endless vault filled with glittering treasures. Mountains of gold, precious gems, and priceless artifacts surrounded her. The promise of unimaginable wealth and opulence was now a tangible reality. Reba revealed in the abundance, the allure of her newfound affluence blinding her to the cost of this apparent utopia.

Her eyes fluttered open to reveal her green irises. Her vision cleared to the sight of Aba. She pulled him into an embrace that pushed him over. She knew it wasn't real. Aba died two winters ago in a fight with Anis' gang. But she would hop on for as long as she could. "I'm a dead child. Let us not prolong the inevitable." She trembled as she pulled back to burn his face into her memory.

"Yes, I know, my child. I know." He nodded his head as he spoke reassuringly at his ward.

"You know, it's quite funny how you think that your greatest desire is riches. It's family. You already have a family," he said with a gentle smile. Tears streamed down her face as she finally uttered the word she never used for him.

"Father!" Aba pulled her in for an embrace one last time.

"My daughter. You are more precious to me than any jewel or coin. I love you. I have always believed in you."

She breathed in his scent. The woody musk calmed her. She would make the sorcerer pay for putting her through this. The scape unraveled and ripped apart like an old and forgotten piece of cloth. Darkness enveloped her as she found herself in the land of the shadows. She felt Ernest was close to her. She would find him and Frederick and they would destroy the sorcerer if it was the last thing she did.

FREDERICK'S DREAM: THE COURT OF NOBILITY AND FORGOTTEN TEARS

In Frederick's dream, he found himself in a grand court, adorned with opulent tapestries and surrounded by admirers. As the noble knight, he was lauded for his chivalry and valor. Here, he held the highest honor, serving as the esteemed protector of Dream Haven. Yet, beneath the veneer of glory, doubts crept in a persistent whisper, questioning the authenticity of his noble deeds.

The knight's deep blue eyes opened with a snap and his hands instinctively grabbed for his sword. "Calm your nerves, boy!" the familiar voice of his gray-bearded master bellowed... only, his beard was not gray. It was salt and pepper. Frederick frowned in confusion. A giggle sounded behind him. He remembered.

The daughters of the more elite would come and watch the spar of the knights. He turned his head. His suspicion was confirmed. Millie, the daughter of Baldwin Geyser, led the group of giggling ladies. Their brightly colored frocks momentarily blinded him.

"Behind you, Fred," she almost whispered.

He ducked in response. Sidestepping Karston, another knight in training. He quickly parried with a swift jab to his face, knocking out his larger opponent. Millie smiled and nodded at him. She pulled out

her embroidered handkerchief and threw it at him before floating away with her flock of brightly colored birds.

He bent to pick up the heavily perfumed handkerchief as he felt a weighty hand on his shoulder. He resumed his fighting stance, swatting away the hand of his master. "Not in this life, boy. Come with me and pick up that girl's clothes," the older knight said with a smirk. He rarely smiled. Frederick's knighting ceremony passed by in a blur two winters after his sparring days.

He would choose if he would walk the path of a Dreamcatcher or a soldier. Feeling a sense of déjà vu, Frederick picked the path of the Dreamcatcher. He knew he had walked the path of a soldier once. He remembered it ended in his shame and indignation.

He donned his Dreamcatcher armor and stepped out into the hall of a new beginning.

Four winters had passed since he became a Dreamcatcher. He had risen the ranks very quickly with many agreeing that he had promised to one day lead the order.

He walked up the stairs of the highest tower of the great hall and glanced at the open court below before moving his eyes across the massive city. His eyes caught the mountains several leagues beyond the walls of the stronghold. A dark splotch caught his eye. He'd never seen it before, but he recognized it. It was the Whispering Woods and he was in a dream conjured by the sorcerer.

The reality dawned on him. He ran down the flight of stairs to find Master Thorn in the training grounds. The man's wide back was facing him. Frederick caught his breath and spoke, "Goodbye. You were the only father I ever had."

Thorn moved his head but did not attempt to leave what he was doing. "I will make you proud," Frederick said with tears welling up in his eyes, cracking his voice at the end. Thorn turned. Tears meeting tears.

The elder nodded. "You've lived trying not to make the same mistakes, offend the same people. Life is not meant to be like that. I am glad I was blessed with another chance to watch you grow. My son." The threatening tear would finally escape from its blue prison. "You have made me proud," he added as the world unraveled before Frederick.

"Well, it's about time," commented Reba's voice. His eyes opened to see a smiling pair. "Did you wait long?" he asked, biting into the joke.

The heroes held hands, drawing from the wells within them and filling them anew with divine power, a bright golden light enveloped the dream.

Together, the trio brandished the divine power and ripped open the escape they were trapped in to find themselves in the large cave-like structure that existed beneath the great hall. Sensing the sorcerer, the heroes readied themselves for battle. The sorcerer weaved the darkness, transporting them into the dream realm.

In the dream realm, the sorcerer manifested as a nightmarish entity, shadows swirling around him like a cloak of malevolence. His eyes glowed with an unholy fervor as he conjured illusions and twisted dreams, attempting to ensnare the heroes' minds. Simultaneously, in the tangible realm, his presence distorted reality, warping the very fabric of the basement.

Ernest, drawing strength from the divine light within his sword, surged forward, determined to sever the sorcerer's hold on both realms. The clash began a dance of divine radiance against the abyss of shadows. Each swing of the sword created shockwaves that reverberated through the dream realm and reality alike.

Reba, in the dream realm, fired arrows infused with mythical energy, seeking to disrupt the sorcerer's illusions. Her aim was true, piercing through the veils of deception, unraveling the nightmares he sought to weave.

In reality, the sorcerer recoiled from the impact of the mythical arrows, his shadowy form flickering momentarily.

Frederick never ceased to overwhelm the sorcerer with heavy hits of his great broadsword at the sorcerer.

The sorcerer, undeterred, unleashed his dark magic, blurring the boundaries between dreams and reality.

Illusions and shadowy figures materialized, complicating the heroes' battle. Reba's bow hummed with ancient power, allowing her to discern the true from the false. Together with Ernest and Frederick, they navigated through the dual onslaught, their movements a synchronized ballet of combat and evasion.

As the battle unfolded, the great hall itself seemed to respond to the clash of powers. Reality wavered, creating a harmony of shifting landscapes. One moment, the heroes fought within a dreamlike forest,

the next, they stood atop towering cliffs overlooking a vast abyss. The sorcerer manipulated the very environment, turning the battle into a surreal weave between realms.

Ernest, most attuned to the divine forces coursing through him, focused on shattering the illusions within the dream realm. His sword cut through the deceptive mirages, revealing the sorcerer's true form. Simultaneously, in the tangible world, Reba's arrows found their mark, piercing through the sorcerer's shadowy defenses.

The sorcerer, sensing the build-up of divine and mythical energies, unleashed a surge of darkness. Reality itself seemed to quake as the heroes grappled with the overwhelming force. In a desperate maneuver, Ernest and Reba combined their powers, creating a barrier of divine light and mythical energy that repelled the encroaching darkness.

The battle reached its zenith as the heroes pressed forward, determined to confront the sorcerer at the heart of the great hall. The sorcerer, however, unleashed his ultimate gambit—an amalgamation of nightmares and illusions that blurred the line between dream and reality.

In the dream realm, the heroes faced manifestations of their deepest fears, twisted and amplified by the sorcerer's dark influence. Reality, too, warped around them, mirroring the horrors of the dream realm. Yet, fueled by their unwavering resolve, they confronted the nightmarish spectacles with a shared determination.

Now, with the sorcerer's newfound power, he rained a barrage of inky black shadow on the heroes. He focused on Reba, who was the most irksome to him. With her distracted, he could focus on the knight and the boy. Little did he know, however, that the decision would cost him the sword.

In one last effort to hunt the sorcerer, Reba channeled a great deal of divine power into her next arrow, risking her life. The arrow exploded with a massive shockwave of light and fire weakening their adversary momentarily.

Within that daze, Frederick blinked to the sorcerer's face, grabbed him, and threw him across the stone hall. Ernest, wasting no time, propelled himself into the air, colliding with the sorcerer.

"No! You will never defeat me. You are but lesser forms that merely stumbled upon divinity." He looked closely at the trio, now standing together. The sword gleamed in the hands of the boy. Confused, the sorcerer slowly looked to his hand that once held the sword to find it missing. His head whipped about, frantically searching for his hand.

Seeing his vulnerability, the trio attacked in unison, furiously pushing the sorcerer back. One lady attempted as a fail-safe.

He unleashed shadows at them, hoping to run. As the battle

raged, the trio channeled the divine power to unravel the sorcerer's enchantments. Standing together, the trio proved to be much too powerful for him to handle. He had underestimated them more than ever. Their bond proved solid, and their training was fresh in their memories.

They rained assault upon an assault upon the sorcerer, pushing him back steadily. The illusions that had ensnared Dream Haven began to dissipate like morning mist. The shadows retreated, unable to withstand the radiant force of the heroes' combined strength.

The sorcerer was scared. Fear raked through his ancient body like chills. The boy blinked to appear before him. Looking at him now, his black eyes remembered the first hero. They looked alike. The same dark hair and determined eyes glared at him.

Ernest sucked in a breath as he raised the sword. In a swift movement, he cut off the head of the sorcerer. The body only fell seconds after the head rolled to the floor. He watched as the body turned to dust.

"Ugh. So, that's what thousand-year-old blood looks like," Frederick said with a grimace. Reba mirrored his expression. Ernest swung the sword, flicking the inky blood from the glistening blade.

As the sorcerer's powers waned, he vanished into the abyss, leaving Dream Haven bathed in the pure light of truth and liberation. The once-enchanted realm awakened from its prolonged slumber, and the inhabitants, no longer shackled by illusions, embraced a newfound sense of freedom.

He glanced at the blade as they made their way to the great hall above. The sword hummed in gratitude, sending images of the millennia it lay in the stony prison. An old woman stood before the several tied-up elites who knelt beside her.

"My name is Atlanta." Her voice was loud and confident. Her tattered clothes were surely a garment of her status.

"You are the ones who saved us. We all saw you in the dream."

She bowed deeply in gratitude and continued her address. "These men sided with the sorcerer." She gestured to the kneeling men. "What

shall we do with them?" The heroes shared a look, agreeing to let Frederick handle this. He was better suited to matters of speech.

The aftermath of the battle was horrendous. The city lay in ruin. Many died. Some thought that the ones who died were non-dreamers, knowing that the toll of the spell was too great for their bodies. In contrast, many dreamers also died. The city's population was halved.

The group of traitors Atlanta captured were swiftly executed. There was no time for sentiment. There was too much work to be done with no objection. Most of the elite tried to object to Frederick leading the city but were quickly silenced. Atlanta reminded them that politics would only keep them back from growing.

She also made it clear that none of them could even hope to defy him anyway, which he proved when he executed the traitors with one fell swoop of his great sword of light.

Frederick, along with Atlanta and her small group, organized the rebuild. All they did was clear the rubble, but in due time, the city of Dream Haven would return back to its former glory.

The future of Dream Haven was uncertain as was that of the dreamscapes. They both lay in ruin. But with the defeat of the evil sorcerer and his cohorts, all now had access to the dreamscapes. The old reign of the Dreamcatchers was also over. No more would any man, woman, or group seek to play as gods.

Ernest journeyed back to the Whispering Woods to return the sword like he had promised. Reba decided to accompany him. They had the option of dreamwalking but chose to use the northern gate and pass through dwarfish territory instead. They had both longed to see the world, and this proved to be the perfect excuse.

Once they returned the sword, they'd hurry back. More than seeing the world, the most important thing for the trio was the future of Dream Haven. A wonderful future where all could dream and live as they wanted.

And it wasn't far-fetched.

Baron staggered in the wet marshlands beside Dream Haven. It was not so hard to escape the crude ties that kept him. He cursed Atlanta for keeping him in such a pitiful state. He would return, he vowed.

At least he vowed to first make it out of the bog. His feet moving slowly as he tried to navigate the marsh. He did not know where he was going, he just tried to head in a general east direction.

Once it was night, he would fetch the supplies he stashed in dreamscapes and survive on that. He recalled the battle within the city. He sensed that his lord was fighting and losing, so he started to plan. He had first stashed water, then some food from the stores of his mansion.

Gregor, the imbecile, kept troubling him about what he was doing. He didn't have the energy to answer him. He did not also feel any regret leaving him to die at the hands of the half-born called Frederick. He ran for his life.

He swatted a number of mosquitoes that fed on his open skin. His anger burning against them as the sun was beginning to set.

He waddled slowly as he planned his revenge. He had books on necromancy and hoped to resurrect his master. Except that, now, he would control him.

He smiled at the thought of controlling a being so powerful. He would also aim for the stars. If he could strike the weakened city of Dream Haven and perhaps gather many nightmares and shadow creatures, maybe he could win. Perhaps he too could become the new God of Dreams. He laughed to himself.

It was almost sunset now as the mosquitoes' assault

intensified. He angrily used both hands to wave them away. "Just you wait," he said to himself.

The sun had set now. He was alone momentarily, unsure what to make of the sudden silence. He took a step. And then another. Feeling safe, he continued.

A loud gurgle rose from beneath him as the mud around him started to bubble and almost boil. Suddenly, more mosquitoes came at him in a cloud. At the same time, hundreds of snakes jumped at him from the muddy depths below.

In less than a minute, a hollow husk of what was once human remained still clothed in the dazzling silk and velvet.

ABOUT THE AUTHOR

Callie A. Viera is known for her captivating storytelling and
unique world-building. Born and raised in South Dakota, she has
always been fascinated by the power of imagination and its ability
to transport readers into different realms.

Her passion for writing was ignited at a young age, and she has
since dedicated her life to creating enchanting tales that resonate
with readers of all ages. Her book, "Sword of Forgotten Dreams,"
is a testament to her creativity and love for fantasy literature.

Viera's work goes beyond mere entertainment. She uses her
stories to explore complex themes such as courage, friendship,
and self-discovery. Her characters are engaging and relatable,
making it easy for readers to connect with them on a deeper level.

www.ingramcontent.com/pod-product-compliance
Lightning Source LLC
Chambersburg PA
CBHW061454150726
47987CB00001B/449